T0197258

YASUNARI KAWABATA

THE DANCING GIRL OF IZU

AND OTHER STORIES

OTHER BOOKS BY YASUNARI KAWABATA

YASUNARI KAWABATA

THE DANCING GIRL OF IZU

AND OTHER STORIES

Translated by J. Martin Holman

COUNTERPOINT
BERKELEY

LIBRARY OF CONGRESS CATALOGING-IN-PUBLICATION DATA
Kawabata, Yasunari, 1899–1972.
  The dancing girl of Izu and other stories / Yasunari Kawabata;
translated by J. Martin Holman.
  1. Kawabata, Yasunari, 1899–1972—Translations into English.
1. Holman, J. Martin. II. Title.
PL832.A9A25   1997
895.6'344—dc21

ISBN 10: 1-887178-94-5
ISBN 13: 978-1-887178-94-5

Book design by Caroline McEver
Cover design by Amy Evans McClure

COUNTERPOINT
2560 Ninth Street Suite 318
Berkeley, CA 94710
www.counterpointpress.com

Printed in the United States of America

Contents

TRANSLATOR'S NOTE

In 1925, Yasunari Kawabata published one of the most enduring and appealing works of modern Japanese literature. "The Dancing Girl of Izu" takes up themes that would occupy Kawabata for the rest of his life. The story is filled with a longing—a longing that borders on anxiety—to be loved and to love what may be unattainable. The young man in the story also yearns for purity and beauty, as many of Kawabata's older characters would later do in *Snow Country* and other works, perhaps only vaguely aware that the realization of his desire would mean the end of the virginal object of his passion. While still a student, Kawabata himself had made such a walking trip down the Izu Peninsula, southwest of Tokyo. Later, after he had published the story, he continued to seek comfort and inspiration amid the mountains and hot springs of Izu, living there for some years.

Born in Osaka in 1899, Kawabata had lost both his father and mother by the time he was three years old, his grandmother when he was eight, and his older sister not long thereafter. His last close living relative, his blind grandfather with whom he lived, died when Kawabata was fourteen years old. Many of Kawabata's

works from the 1920s take up the loss of family. Fearful
that the sorrow of his childhood and youth may have
warped his personality, Kawabata probed his memory
in autobiographical stories like "Oil" and "Gathering
Ashes," only to discover he could not trust it. Unlike
so many of his contemporaries, who devoted themselves
to the supposed sincerity and confessional realism of
the first-person novel, Kawabata was either unable or
unwilling to fix borders in the regions where memory
merges with dream and desire. He seemed content to
allow imagination to reshape the past, as he may have
done in "Diary of My Sixteenth Year" and certainly did
in "The Dancing Girl of Izu."

In the 1920s Kawabata emerged as a proponent of
the Shinkankakuha, the "New Perception" School.
Although his puzzling ellipses, abrupt transitions, and
occasionally jarring juxtapositions of images suggest the
influence of European modernism, all of these features
are also to be found in the classical literature of Japan,
which Kawabata held in great reverence. Kawabata's
stated desire as a "New Perceptionist" in the 1920s—to
"see the world with new eyes"—was tempered by his
devotion to the beauty of Japan's past. In almost fifty
years of writing, Kawabata produced more than 140
very short works of fiction that demonstrate his new/old
vision, a unique contribution to Japanese literature that
he called "palm-of-the-hand stories," most of which are
only two or three pages long.

Some of the stories involve fantastic or surreal ele-
ments derived from Japanese legend and folklore. "The
Princess of the Dragon Palace" plays on the popular
old story of Urashima Taro, who was taken to a magi-
cal realm beneath the sea on the back of a turtle and,
returning to land, found that hundreds of years had

passed in his absence. "Horse Beauty" contains echoes of a lesser-known tale of Chinese origin about a girl who falls in love with a white horse and is carried away to heaven wrapped in the animal's flailed skin after her father discovers the affair and kills the horse. Other stories are not so obviously indebted to traditional tales.

During the 1920s, Kawabata focused much energy on his palm-of-the-hand stories, testing the emotional and aesthetic capacity of the form. He crafted his later, longer works by linking, after the manner of traditional poetry, the kind of brief, evocative scenes he perfected in these palm-sized works. The eighteen stories in section two of this volume and "Gathering Ashes" in section one represent almost all of the previously untranslated palm-of-the-hand stories that Kawabata wrote before 1930.

I am grateful to be able to offer this first unabridged English translation of Kawabata's "The Dancing Girl of Izu," along with other early stories from his first decade of writing. Kawabata has been described as an "eternal traveler." His literary journey began here.

■ ■ ■

Many friends and colleagues read these translations and offered suggestions. I am indebted to Professor Van C. Gessel of Brigham Young University, without whose help the dancing girl and I might have both missed the boat. I offer my thanks to author and professor Marilyn Sides of Wellesley College for her thoughtful reading of the man-uscript and perceptive comments, and to students at the Associated Kyoto Program Center at Doshisha University in Japan for their suggestions. I wish to thank colleague Miwako Okigami for answers to my questions. I also offer thanks to my friends Mari Kitaoka and Makoto and Fumi

Higashinoya, who taught me much about Japan, and to my students in literature classes at Gettysburg College, whose helpful comments on earlier versions of some of these stories were more pointed and courageous than their teacher had expected. I am grateful for the bilingual skills of my two older children, Katherine and Ethan, who demonstrated that all those years they spent in Japanese public schools had finally paid off in their being able to help their father with his work, thus setting examples for their younger siblings, Amanda and Jordan. And finally, I thank my wife, Susan James Holman, for her loving encouragement, editorial insight, and good judgment.

■■■

This translation is dedicated to my parents, James M. and Betty Sue Embery Holman.

J. Martin Holman
Gettysburg, June 1997

■■■

In the year since the publication of the cloth edition of this book, I have received suggestions for revisions from friends and colleagues, some of which I have incorporated in this paperback edition. In particular I would like to thank Mark Morris of Cambridge University for his thoughtful suggestions for improvements in the translation and Ge-ling Shang of Gettysburg College for help with Buddist terminology.

JMH
London, Ontario, Canada, July 1998

ONE

THE DANCING GIRL OF IZU

1

About the time the road began to wind and I realized that I was finally near Amagi Pass, a curtain of rain swept up after me at a terrific speed from the foot of the mountain, painting the dense cedar forests white.

I was twenty years old. I wore my school cap, *hakama* over my indigo-dyed kimono, and carried a student's bag over my shoulder. It was the fourth day of my solitary journey down the Izu Peninsula. I had stayed at Shuzenji Hot Spring one night, then two nights at Yugashima. And now, wearing high clogs, I was climbing Amagi. Although I had been enchanted by the layers upon layers of mountains, the virgin forests, and the shades of autumn in the deep valleys, I was hurrying along this road, my chest pounding with a certain expectation. Before long, great drops of rain began to pelt me, and I bolted up the steep, twisted road. I was relieved to reach the teahouse on the north side of the pass at last, but stopped short in the doorway. My expectation had been realized all too splendidly. The troupe of itinerant performers was inside, taking a rest.

As soon as the dancing girl noticed me standing there, she pulled out the cushion she had been kneeling on, turned it over, and placed it near her.

"Yes." That's all I said before I sat down. The words "thank you" stuck in my throat. I was out of breath from running up the road and from my astonishment.

Sitting so close, facing the dancing girl, I fumbled to pull a cigarette from my kimono sleeve. The girl took the ashtray sitting in front of her female companion and placed it near me. Naturally, I did not speak.

The dancing girl looked to be about seventeen years old. Her hair was arranged elaborately in an unusual old style unfamiliar to me. Although it made her striking oval face look quite small, it created a beautiful harmony. She gave the impression of the girls from illustrations in old romances who were depicted with an emphasis on their extravagant hair. The dancing girl was accompanied by a woman in her forties, two older girls, and a man of about twenty-five, who was wearing a jacket with the insignia of Nagaoka Hot Springs on it.

I had seen this troupe twice previously. The first time I encountered them, near Yugawa Bridge, I was on my way to Yugashima Hot Springs while they were going to Shuzenji. There were three girls in the group. The dancing girl was carrying a drum. After we passed, I looked back at them again and again. I had finally experienced the romance of travel. Then, my second night at Yugashima, the entertainers had come to the inn to perform. Sitting halfway down the ladderlike stairs, I had gazed intently at the girl as she danced on the wooden floor of the entryway.

"If they were at Shuzenji the other day and Yugashima tonight, then they would probably go to Yugano

Springs on the south side of Amagi Pass tomorrow. Surely I could catch up with them along the fifteen miles of mountain road over Amagi." Thus I had been daydreaming as I hastened along the road that day. Now we had ended up taking shelter from the rain at the same teahouse. My heart was pounding.

In a moment the old woman who ran the teahouse led me to another room. It appeared it was not used regularly and had no sliding paper doors. When I peered down into the magnificent valley outside the window, I could scarcely see the bottom. It gave me goose bumps. My teeth chattered and I shivered. The old woman came back to serve tea. I told her I felt cold.

"You're all wet, aren't you, sir?" She spoke with great deference. "Come in here for a while. Dry your clothes." Reaching for my hand, she led me into her own parlor.

There was a hearth in the middle of the floor of her room. When she opened the sliding door, the hot air flowed out. I stood at the threshold, hesitating. An old man sat cross-legged by the fire, his body pale and swollen like a drowning victim. He turned his languid eyes toward me. They were yellowed to the pupils as if putrefied. Around him lay piles of old letters and scraps of paper. They almost buried him. I stood stiff, staring at him, wondering how he could be alive, this mystery in the mountains.

"I'm embarrassed to have you see him this way. Don't worry. This is my old husband. He may be unsightly, but he can't move. Please be patient with him."

After thus apologizing, the old woman explained that her husband had suffered from palsy for many years and now his whole body was almost paralyzed. The mountains of papers were actually correspondence from every possible source describing treatments for palsy and packets of medicine the old man had ordered from throughout the country. Whenever he heard of a treatment from travelers who came over the pass or saw an advertisement in the newspaper, he never failed to send for it. He kept the papers around him in heaps, staring at them, never disposing of a single one. Through the years he had accumulated mountains of aging scraps of paper.

Without a word to the old woman, I bent over the hearth. An automobile navigating the pass rattled the house. I wondered why the old man did not move down to a lower elevation, with the autumn already this cold and snow soon to cover the pass. Steam rose from my kimono. The fire was hot enough to scorch my face. The old woman went back out to the shop, commenting to one of the female entertainers.

"So this is the little girl you had with you before. She's turned out to be such a nice girl. That's good for you. How pretty she's become. Girls grow up so fast."

About an hour later, I heard the entertainers preparing to leave. I had not settled in to stay either, but I was so anxious that I did not have the courage to stand up. Although they were seasoned travelers, they would be walking at a woman's pace, so I was certain I could catch up even if I left a mile or so behind them. Still, I grew impatient sitting by the hearth. Once the entertainers had left, my daydreams began a vivid, reckless dance. The old woman returned from seeing the entertainers off.

"Where are they staying tonight?" I asked.

"There's no way to tell where people like that are going to stay, is there, young man? Wherever they can attract an audience, that's where they stay. It doesn't matter where it might be. I don't think the likes of them would have a place already planned."

The scorn that lurked in the woman's words so stirred me, I thought to myself: If that is true, then I'll have the dancing girl stay in my room tonight.

The rain abated and the mountain peak cleared. The old woman tried to detain me longer, telling me the sky would be completely cloudless if only I would wait ten more minutes. But I just could not remain sitting there.

"Please take care of yourself," I said to the old man. "It's going to get colder." I spoke from my heart as I stood up. His yellow eyes lolled in his head, and he gave a slight nod.

"Sir! Sir!" The old woman followed me outside. "This is far too much money. I just can't accept it." She picked up my bag in both hands and refused to give it to me. She would not listen, no matter how much I tried to dissuade her. The old woman told me she would accompany me up the road a bit. She repeated the same words as she tottered along behind me for a hundred yards.

"This is much too generous. I'm sorry we didn't serve you better. I'll make certain to remember your face. When you pass this way again, we'll do something special for you. Be sure to stop by next time. I won't forget you."

She seemed so overwhelmed, as if she were on the verge of tears, just because I had left a fifty-sen coin. But I was eager to catch up with the dancers, and the old woman's doddering pace hindered me. At last we reached the tunnel at the pass.

"Thank you very much," I said. "You'd better go back now. Your husband is there all alone." The old woman finally released my bag.

Cold drops of water plopped inside the dark tunnel. Up ahead, the tiny portal to southern Izu grew brighter.

2

The mountain road, stitched on one side with white-washed pickets, coursed down from the mouth of the tunnel like a jagged lightning bolt. The scene resembled a landscape in miniature. I could make out the itinerant entertainers down at the bottom. Before I had walked half a mile, I overtook them. It would be too obvious were I to slacken my pace too abruptly, so I nonchalantly passed the women. When the man, who was walking about twenty yards ahead of the others, noticed me, he paused.

"You walk fast. . . . We're lucky the weather cleared up," he said.

Relieved, I fell into step with the man. He asked me all kinds of questions. Seeing the two of us talking, the women scurried to join us.

The man was carrying a large wicker trunk on his back. The woman in her forties was holding a puppy. The oldest girl was toting a cloth bundle. The middle girl also had a wicker trunk. Everyone carried something. The dancing girl had a drum and frame on her back. Little by little, the woman, who seemed to be in her forties, began to talk to me.

"He's an upper-school student," the oldest girl whispered to the dancing girl. When I looked around she smiled. "That's right, isn't it? I know that much. Students are always coming down to the island."

They were from the harbor town of Habu on Oshima, the largest island off the southern tip of the Izu Peninsula. They had been on the road since leaving the island in the spring, but it was turning cold and they had not yet made preparations for winter. They said they were planning to stay in Shimoda for just ten days, then cross over to the island from Ito Hot Springs. At the mention of Oshima, I felt even more the poetry of the situation. Again I glanced at the dancing girl's lovely hair. I asked questions about Oshima.

"A lot of students come to the island to swim, don't they?" the dancing girl said to the girl with her.

I turned back toward them. "In the summer, right?"

The dancing girl was flustered. "In the winter, too," I thought I heard her answer softly.

"In the winter, too?" I asked.

The dancing girl simply looked at her companion and giggled.

"You can swim in the winter, too?" I asked again. The dancing girl blushed. She nodded, with a serious look.

"This girl is such a silly one," the older woman laughed.

The road to Yugano ran about eight miles down through the valley of the Kawazu River. On this side of the pass, even the mountains and the color of the sky began to look more southern. As the man and I continued our conversation, we took a liking to each other. We passed tiny villages with names like Oginori and Nashimoto. About the time the thatched roofs of Yugano came into view at the foot of the mountain, I ventured to tell the man that I wanted to travel with them to Shimoda. He seemed delighted.

When we arrived at a cheap lodging house in Yugano, the older woman nodded as if to say good-bye. But the man spoke for me: "This young gentleman has kindly offered to accompany us."

"Well, well. As the old saying goes, 'On the road, a traveling companion; and in the world, kindness.' Even boring people like us will help you pass the time. Come on in and take a rest." She spoke without formality. The girls all glanced at me at the same time. They stopped talking, their faces seemingly indifferent. Then their gaze turned to embarrassment.

I went upstairs with them and put down my bag. The woven floor mats and sliding panel doors were old and dirty. The dancing girl brought us some tea from downstairs. Kneeling in front of me, she blushed bright red. Her hands were trembling. The teacup almost tumbled off the saucer. She set it down on the mat to keep it from falling but spilled the whole cup of tea. I was amazed at her bashfulness.

"My goodness. She's started thinking about the opposite sex. How disgusting! Look at that!" The older woman furrowed her brow in dismay and threw a hand towel at the girl, who picked it up and wiped the mat, looking ill at ease.

Caught off guard by the woman's words, I reconsidered my feelings. The daydream that the old woman at the pass had sparked in me had been dashed.

"The young student's indigo kimono certainly is nice," the woman remarked, her eyes fixed on me. "The pattern is the same as Tamiji's. Isn't it? Isn't it the same?"

After pressing the girls several times, she spoke to me. "We have another child at home still in school. I was thinking of him. He has the same kind of kimono as yours. These days indigo kimonos are so expensive, I just don't know what to do."

"What kind of school?"

"Elementary school, fifth grade."

"Oh, you have a fifth grader? . . . "

"His school is not on Oshima. It's in Kofu. We've been on Oshima for a long time, but Kofu is our original home."

After we rested for an hour, the man led me to another

hot spring inn. Until then I had assumed I would be staying at the same lodging house with the entertainers. We walked about one hundred yards along a gravel road and down some stone steps, then crossed a bridge near a public bath beside a stream. The garden of the inn was on the other side of the bridge.

I stepped into the bath and the man got in after me. He told me he was twenty-four. His wife had lost two children, one by miscarriage and one that was born prematurely. I assumed he was from Nagaoka, since his jacket bore a Nagaoka Hot Springs emblem. His intellectual manner of speaking and his facial expressions made me wonder if he had been following the entertainers and carrying their luggage simply out of curiosity, or perhaps because he had fallen in love with one of them.

I ate lunch as soon as I got out of the bath. I had left Yugashima at eight o'clock in the morning, but it was not yet three o'clock now.

As the man made his way to the inn gate, he looked up at my window to say good-bye.

"Buy yourself some persimmons or something. I'm sorry. This is such a rude way to give this to you, from the second floor." I tossed down a packet of money. The man refused it and turned to go, but he couldn't leave the money lying in the garden so he returned and picked it up.

"You shouldn't do things like this," he said, tossing the packet back up at me. It landed on the thatched roof. When I threw it down a second time, he took it with him.

Rain started pouring around sunset. The mountains turned colorless and lost their depth. The small stream in front of the inn ran yellow as I watched it. The sound of rushing water grew louder. Thinking that the dancers would never come looking for customers in this torrent, I could not sit still, so I went to the bath two or three more times. My room was dismal. An electric light hung in a square hole cut in the wall between my room and the next, where it could illuminate both rooms.

"Ton, ton, ton, ton." In the distance beyond the clamor of the rain, the vague reverberations of a drum arose. I shoved open one of the shutters and hung out the window. The drum seemed to be getting closer. The rain and wind lashed my head. Closing my eyes and straining to hear, I tried to determine the path of the drum as it approached. A moment later I heard the sound of a samisen. I heard a woman's long scream. I heard boisterous laughter. I surmised that the entertainers had been called to the banquet room at the inn across from their own. I could distinguish two or three women's voices and three or four men's. I expected them to travel in my direction once the party broke up, but it seemed the party would pass the point of merry drinking and dissolve into riotous nonsense. Occasionally a woman's high, piercing voice rent the night like a thunderbolt. My nerves were on edge. I left the shutter open and just sat by the window. I felt some consolation every time I heard the drum.

"Oh, the dancing girl is still at the party. She's sitting, playing the drum."

I could not bear the silences when the drum stopped. I sank down into the depths of the sound of the rain.

At length I could hear the noise of confused footsteps—were they playing tag or dancing in circles? Then all fell silent. I opened my eyes wide, trying to peer through the darkness. What was this stillness? I was tormented, wondering if the dancing girl's night might be sullied.

I closed the shutters and crawled into bed, but my
chest felt heavy. I went down again for a bath. I thrashed
the water. The rain stopped and the moon came out.
The autumn night was bright, washed clean by the rain.
I slipped out of the bathhouse barefoot, but I could not
do anything. It was past two o'clock.

3

After nine o'clock the next morning, the man from the
troupe called on me at my inn. I had just awakened, so I
invited him along to the bath. It was a cloudless, almost
springlike day in southern Izu. The water had risen in
the stream beside the inn and reflected the warm sun.
My previous night's anguish seemed like a dream. Still,
I broached the subject with the man.

"You were having quite a time last night. The drum
was going until late."

"What? You could hear it?"

"Yes, I could."

"It was for some local folks. They make such a racket.
It's not much fun."

He appeared unconcerned, so I said no more.

"Look. They're over at the other bath. I think they've
noticed us. They're laughing."

He pointed across the stream toward the public bath
on the other side. I could distinguish seven or eight
bodies through the steam.

Suddenly a naked woman ran out from the rear of the
dark bathhouse. She stood at the edge of the changing
area as if she might come flying down the bank. She
was shouting with her arms outstretched. She was stark

naked, without even a towel. It was the dancing girl. When I gazed at her white body, legs stretched, standing like a young paulownia tree, I felt pure water flowing through my heart. I breathed a sigh of relief and laughed out loud. She's a child—a child who can run out naked in broad daylight, overcome with joy at finding me, and stand tall on her tiptoes. I kept laughing with delight. My head was clear as though wiped clean. I could not stop smiling.

The dancing girl's hair had been arranged too elaborately for her age. She had looked seventeen or eighteen. What's more, she had been dressed like a young woman in her prime. I had made a ridiculous mistake.

After I returned to my room with the man, the oldest girl came to the garden at my inn and stood looking at the chrysanthemum bed. The dancing girl had stopped halfway across the bridge. The older woman came out of the public bath and glanced over at the two of them. The dancing girl smiled and shrugged her shoulders at me as if to indicate that she would be scolded if she didn't go back. She hurried away.

The older woman walked out as far as the bridge and called to me. "Please come visit us."

"Please come visit us," the oldest girl repeated. Then they left. However, the man stayed until late afternoon.

That evening I was playing go with a traveling paper wholesaler when I heard a drum in the garden. I started to get up. "Some entertainers have come looking for customers."

"What? Them? They're nothing. Well, then it's your turn. I put my stone here." The paper seller pointed at the board, intent on the game. But now I was restless. It sounded as though the entertainers were leaving. The man called from the garden.

"Good night."

I went out to the window in the hall and motioned for them to come up. The entertainers whispered among themselves in the garden, then walked around to the entrance.

"Good evening." After the man, the three girls each bowed to the two of us, kneeling on the floor like geisha. It suddenly became apparent that I had lost the go game.

"There doesn't appear to be any way out. I give up."

"You think so? I think I'm the one who's on the short side. Either way, it's close."

The paper dealer kept playing, studying the board and counting points without even a glance at the enter-tainers. The girls placed their drums and samisen in the corner of the room, then started playing a game of "five-in-a-row" on a Chinese chess board. Meanwhile, I indeed lost the go game that I had previously been winning.

"How about it? One more round, just one more round," the paper dealer pleaded. He was persistent, but I just smiled vacantly. He gave up and left the room.

The girls came over to the go board.

"Are you making the rounds again this evening?" I asked.

"Yes, we are, but . . . " The man looked toward the girls. "What do you think? Shall we just forget about it and have a good time instead?"

"That would be wonderful."

"Won't you get in trouble?"

"What do you mean? We wouldn't find any customers anyway, even if we did make the rounds."

We played "five-in-a-row" and enjoyed ourselves until past midnight.

After the entertainers left, I could not get to sleep.

My mind was so keen. I stepped into the hall and called out, "Hey, Mr. Paper Dealer!"

The man, who was about sixty, sprang out of his room, elated. "It's all night tonight! We're going to play until morning."

Now I, too, felt ready for a good battle.

4

We had agreed to leave Yugano at eight o'clock the next morning. Wearing a hunting cap I had bought at a shop beside the public bath, I stuffed my school cap into the bottom of my bag and walked over to the cheap lodging house on the roadside. The sliding doors were all open on the second floor, so I casually went upstairs. The entertainers were still in bed. I stood in the hall, confused.

Lying at my feet, the dancing girl blushed and quickly covered her face with her hands. She was sharing a futon with the middle girl. She still had on her heavy makeup from the night before. The rouge on her lips and the corners of her eyes was slightly smudged. Her emotional appearance as she lay there touched my heart. She turned away as if to avoid the light. Hiding her face with her hands, she slid out of the covers and knelt in the hall.

"Thank you for last night." She gave a pretty bow. I felt awkward standing over her.

The man was sleeping with the oldest girl. Until then I had had no idea they were a couple.

"Oh, I'm sorry." The older woman spoke, sitting up halfway. "I know we had planned to leave today, but we were told there's to be a big party this evening where we can perform, so we decided to stay one more night. If you have to move on today, we could meet in Shimoda. We've already decided to stay at an inn there called Koshuya. It's easy to find." I felt as though I had been dismissed.

"Why don't you wait and leave tomorrow?" the man spoke up. "As she said, we're staying an extra day. I'm sorry. We'd like to keep you on as a traveling companion. Why don't you go with us tomorrow?"

"Yes. Let's do that," the woman added. "After all, you've come with us this far. I'm sorry we're being so selfish. We'll leave tomorrow, even if it's raining spears outside. The day after tomorrow is the forty-ninth day since the baby died. Since it died while we were on the road, we've been planning all along that we should commemorate the forty-ninth day in Shimoda. We've been hurrying to get there by tomorrow. It's probably not proper for me to tell you so much, but it's like we have some kind of connection to you from a previous life. Would you offer devotions with us the day after tomorrow?"

I decided to delay my departure. I went downstairs and talked with the clerk in the dirty office of the lodging house while I waited for the entertainers. The man came down and invited me to go for a walk with him. Along the road to the south was a beautiful bridge. Leaning against the railing, the man began to tell me more about himself. He had acted in a new-style Kabuki troupe in Tokyo for a time and said he still performed occasionally at the port on Oshima. That explained the sword sheath that stuck out of their luggage like an appendage. He told me he also performed when they entertained at gatherings. The wicker trunk held the costumes they used, as well as pots, dishes, and other household effects.

"It's wretched, the mess I've made of my life. But my older brother in Kofu is doing fine as family heir, keeping up the reputation of the family. So, I would be of no use anyway."

"All along I thought you were from Nagaoka Hot Springs."

"Did you? The oldest girl there with us, she's my wife. She's a year younger than you—nineteen. Our second baby was born prematurely, on the road. It lived just a week. My wife still hasn't recovered her full health. The older woman is her mother. The dancing girl is my own little sister."

"So the fourteen-year-old sister you told me about is? . . ."

"She's the one. Actually, it bothers me; I didn't want my sister to have to live like this, but it's a long story."

Then he told me his name was Eikichi, his wife's was Chiyoko, and his sister's was Kaoru. The other girl, Yuriko, seventeen years old, was the only native of Oshima. She was employed by them. Eikichi stared down at the river shallows. He became sentimental and appeared to be on the brink of tears.

As we walked back, we found the dancing girl, her face washed clean of the white makeup, crouching by the road, petting the puppy on the head. I spoke to her as I started back to my room alone.

"Come on over," I said.

"But, by myself, I . . . "

"So, come with your brother."

"We'll be right there."

Before long Eikichi came to my room.

"Where is everyone?" I asked.

"The old lady is so strict with the girls."

However, we had been playing "five-in-a-row" only

a short while when the girls came across the bridge and upstairs. They bowed politely as always and hesitated, kneeling in the hallway. First, Chiyoko, the oldest, stood up.

"This is my room. Don't be so formal. Come on in," I said.

The entertainers stayed about an hour, then went down to the inn bath. They begged me to come along, but I put them off. I said I would go later since there would be three girls in the bath. Shortly, the dancing girl came back upstairs alone to relay a message from Chiyoko.

"She said to come on down. She'll rinse your shoulders for you."

I did not go. Instead I played "five-in-a-row" with the dancing girl. She was surprisingly good. Earlier, when she had played "winner-stays" against Eikichi and the other girls, she had defeated them all handily. I usually win at "five-in-a-row," but I needed all my skill with her. It was refreshing not to have to make easy moves for her. With just the two of us there, the dancing girl initially sat back, playing her stones from a distance with her arm outstretched. But gradually she forgot herself and hunched over the board, absorbed in the game. Her unnaturally beautiful black hair almost touched my chest. Without warning, she blushed. "Please forgive me. I'll get in trouble." Tossing down her stones, she fled the room. The older woman was standing outside the public bath. Chiyoko and Yuriko rushed out of the bath at my inn and hurried back to their lodging house without coming upstairs.

Again Eikichi stayed at the inn with me from morning until late afternoon. The proprietress, a simple, honest woman, warned me against keeping his company, saying it was a waste to feed a fellow like him.

That evening, when I went to the entertainers' lodging house, I found the dancing girl receiving a samisen lesson from the older woman. She stopped playing when she saw me but resumed after the woman said something to her. Whenever the girl's voice rose as she was singing, the woman reprimanded her. "I told you not so loud."

Eikichi had been called over to the banquet room of the inn on the other side of the road. I could see him across the way. From where I watched, it looked as though he were groaning.

"What's he doing?"

"That? . . . It's chanting from a Noh drama."

"Noh drama? It sounds strange."

"He's a jack-of-all-trades. You never know what he'll do."

A man of about forty who said he was a poulterer was also staying at the lodging house. He opened the partition between the rooms and invited the girls to have dinner with him. The dancing girl took her chopsticks and went over with Yuriko. They picked through the chicken stew that remained after the man had ravaged the pot. As the girls were returning to their own room, the man patted the dancing girl's shoulder. The woman glared at him.

"Hey, don't touch her. She's an innocent virgin."

The dancing girl addressed the man as "uncle" and asked him to read "The Story of the Lord of Mito" to her, but he left immediately. She did not want to ask me directly, so she told the woman that she would like me to read the rest of "The Story of the Lord of Mito" for her. I picked up the book, with a certain expectation in my heart. Just as I hoped, the dancing girl scooted over beside me. Once I began reading, she brought her face close enough to touch my shoulder, her expression serious. Her eyes sparkled as she gazed at my forehead without blinking. It seemed to be her habit when she was being read to. Earlier, I had noticed that she had held her face right beside the poulterer. The dancing girl's most beautiful feature was her sparkling big dark eyes. The curve of her double eyelids was unspeakably lovely. Next was her flowerlike smile. In her case, the word "flowerlike" was absolutely accurate.

A moment later, the maid from the inn came to call for the dancing girl. She put on her costume.

"I'll be back soon, so please wait. And read the rest to me."

Out in the hallway she bowed low.

"I'll return soon."

"Don't sing," the woman said. The dancing girl picked up her drum and nodded slightly. The woman turned back to me. "Her voice is changing now."

The dancing girl knelt properly in the second floor of the restaurant, beating the drum. I could watch her back from the window as though she were in the next room. The sound of the drum set my heart dancing.

"When the drum enters, the party certainly does liven up." The woman was also looking across the way.

Chiyoko and Yuriko went to the same gathering.

About an hour later all four returned.

"This is all we got." The dancing girl dropped some fifty-sen coins from her fist into the older woman's palm. I read "The Story of the Lord of Mito" out loud for a while. Then they talked about the baby that had died while they were on the road. They said the baby was almost as transparent as water at birth and did not even have the strength to cry. Nevertheless, it lived for a week.

My common goodwill—which neither was mere

curiosity nor bore any trace of contempt for their status as itinerant entertainers—seemed to have touched their hearts. Before I knew it, they had decided that I should accompany them to their place on Oshima.

"The house where Grandpa lives would be good. It's big, and it would be quiet if we chased Grandpa out. You could stay as long as you wanted. And you could study." They made this announcement to me after conferring among themselves.

"We have two small houses. The one in the mountains is usually empty."

Moreover, I was to help out during new year holidays when they performed at the port in Habu.

I realized that their sense of the road was not so hardened as I had first supposed. Rather, it was more of a lighthearted attitude that had not lost the scent of the fields. They were bound together by the familial affection you would expect between parent and child or brother and sister. The hired girl, Yuriko, was the only one who was sullen around me. Perhaps she was at the age when a girl is most bashful.

I left their lodging house halfway through the night. The girls came downstairs to see me off. The dancing girl placed my clogs at the door so I could step into them easily. She stuck her head out the gate and looked up at the bright sky.

"Oh, the moon! We'll be in Shimoda tomorrow. How wonderful. We'll have the baby's forty-ninth-day services. Mother will buy me a comb. We'll do all kinds of things! Would you take me to see a movie?"

The port of Shimoda—it had the air of a hometown that the itinerant entertainers who traveled around the hot springs in Izu and Sagami longed for when they were on the road.

5

The entertainers were carrying the same luggage they had hauled through Amagi Pass. The puppy rested his paws on the woman's arm, looking like a seasoned traveler. Just outside Yugano we found ourselves again in the mountains. The sun hanging over the sea warmed the slopes. We gazed toward the morning sun. Kawazu Beach spread wide in the sunlight out where the Kawazu River flowed.

"That's Oshima over there, isn't it?" I said.

"Of course it is. See how big it looks. Please do come," the dancing girl said.

Perhaps the autumn sky was too dazzling; the sea near the sun looked misted over as it is in the spring. It was another twelve-mile walk from there to Shimoda. For a while the ocean was blocked from view. Chiyoko began to sing a carefree song.

Along the way I was asked whether I preferred to take the main road, which was easier, or a steep path over the mountains that was well over a mile shorter. Naturally I chose the shortcut.

It was an abrupt climb through the trees. I feared we would slip on the fallen leaves. I got so winded that, half in desperation, I pressed down on my knees with the palms of my hands to pick up my pace. Every time I glanced back, the others had fallen farther behind until I could only hear their voices among the trees, except for the dancing girl, who was holding up her skirts and trudging along behind me. She was trailing me by about two yards, neither trying to close the distance between us nor dropping farther back. When I turned and spoke to her, she paused as if startled, then smiled and replied. When she spoke to me, I waited, to give her a chance to catch up. But I should have known that she would stop short and refuse to take a step until I did. When the path twisted and grew even steeper, I quickened my pace again and found the dancing girl climbing intently, as always, just a couple of yards behind me. The mountains were still. The rest of the group was so far behind I could no longer hear them talking.

"Where is your house in Tokyo?"

"My home isn't Tokyo. I live in the school dormitory there."

"I know about Tokyo. I went there to dance during the cherry blossom season. . . . I was little then, so I don't remember anything about it." Then she went on. "Do you have a father?" "Have you ever been to Kofu?" She asked all kinds of questions. We talked about going to see a movie when we got to Shimoda, and again about the dead baby.

We emerged at the mountaintop. The dancing girl placed her drum on a bench in the dry grass and wiped the perspiration from her face with a handkerchief. She started to brush the dust from her legs, then suddenly crouched at my feet and began to brush the hem of my *hakama*. I jerked away, and she dropped to her knees with a thud. She brushed the dust all the way around my kimono, then dropped the hem. I stood there breathing deeply.

"Sit down," she said.

A flock of small birds appeared beside the bench. It was so still I could hear the dry leaves on the branches rustle when they alighted.

"Why do you walk so fast?"

She looked flushed. I thumped the drum with my fingers and the birds flew away.

"I'm thirsty," I said.

"I'll go see if I can find some water."

But shortly the girl came back empty-handed through the grove of yellow trees.

"What do you do on Oshima?"

The dancing girl mentioned two or three girl's names and began talking about something I could not follow. She seemed to be describing Kofu, not Oshima. Apparently the names were her friends at the elementary school she had attended until second grade. The dancing girl just rambled on.

We had waited about ten minutes when the three younger people reached the top. The older woman arrived another ten minutes after them.

On the way down, Eikichi and I purposely hung back, talking at leisure. When we had walked about two hundred yards, the dancing girl came back up from below.

"There's a spring further down. They said you should hurry down. They're waiting until you get there to take a drink."

When I heard they had found water, I ran. Fresh water sprang from between some large rocks in the shade of the trees. The girls stood waiting around the spring.

"Please, you go first," the woman said. "The water will get all cloudy if we put our hands in. You'd think it was too dirty after us women."

I scooped up the cold water in my hands and drank. The women lingered. They wrung out some damp hand towels and wiped themselves.

When we rejoined the Shimoda Highway at the foot of the mountain, we saw several threads of smoke from charcoal-burning huts. We sat down to rest on some timber stacked by the roadside. The dancing girl crouched on the road combing the puppy's shaggy fur with her pink comb.

"The teeth will break," the woman warned her.

"It's okay. I'll get a new one in Shimoda."

Ever since our stay in Yugano, I had been hoping to be given the comb she wore in the front of her hair as a memento, so I did not want her using it on the dog, either.

Eikichi and I spotted bundles of thin bamboo piled by the roadside. Remarking that it would be perfect for walking sticks, we reached them ahead of the others. Following on our heels, the dancing girl located a thick piece taller than she was.

"What are you going to do with it?" Eikichi asked.

She seemed puzzled for a moment, then held it out to me. "Here. It's a walking stick. I pulled out the thickest one."

"You can't do that. If someone sees him with the thickest one, they'll know we stole it. We don't want to get caught. Put it back," Eikichi said.

The dancing girl returned the bamboo pole and caught up with us. This time she handed me a piece of bamboo about the size of my middle finger. Then she threw herself flat on her back on the path between the rice paddies beside the road. Breathing heavily, she waited for the other women.

Eikichi and I walked together as before, this time ten or twelve yards ahead.

"It wouldn't be hard to pull them and replace them with gold teeth."

I turned around when I overheard the dancing girl's voice. She was walking with Chiyoko. The older woman and Yuriko were a short distance behind them. The dancing girl did not appear to notice me looking back.

I heard Chiyoko reply. "That's right. Why don't you tell him."

I gathered they were talking about me. Chiyoko had probably commented that my teeth were crooked, so the dancing girl had suggested gold teeth. They were discussing my looks, yet it did not bother me. I felt so close to them that I did not even care to eavesdrop. They continued their conversation for a time. Then I caught the dancing girl's voice again.

"He's a nice person."

"You're right. He seems like a nice person."

"He really *is* nice. It's good to have such a nice person around."

This exchange had an echo of simplicity and frankness. Hers was a child's voice expressing her sentiments without censure. I, too, was able to meekly consider myself a nice person. Refreshed, I lifted my eyes and surveyed the brilliant mountains. I felt a vague pain behind my eyelids. Twenty years old, I had embarked on this trip to Izu heavy with resentment that my personality had been permanently warped by my orphan's complex and that I would never be able to overcome a stifling melancholy. So I was inexpressibly grateful to find that I looked like a nice person as the world defines the word. The mountains looked bright because we were by the ocean near Shimoda. I swung my bamboo walking stick back and forth, lopping off the heads of the autumn grasses.

Here and there along the way stood signs as we entered villages.

"Beggars and itinerant entertainers — KEEP OUT."

6

Koshuya, a cheap lodging house, was located just within

Shimoda on the north side. I followed the entertainers into a second-floor room that had all the appearances of an attic. There was no ceiling, and when I sat near the windowsill, facing the road, my head almost touched the roof.

"Do your shoulders hurt?" the woman kept asking the dancing girl. "Do your hands hurt?"

The dancing girl moved her hands in the graceful gestures she used when playing the drum. "No, they don't. I can play. I can."

"Well, I'm glad to hear that."

I hefted her drum. "Hey, that's heavy."

"It's heavier than you thought, . . . heavier than that bag of yours." The dancing girl laughed.

The entertainers heartily greeted the other people staying at the inn. Naturally, they were all entertainers and carnival people. Shimoda appeared to be a temporary roost for these birds of passage. The dancing girl gave a copper coin to one of the innkeeper's children who came toddling into the room. When I stood up to leave Koshuya, the dancing girl hurried down ahead of me to the entryway and set my clogs out for me.

"Please be sure to take me to a movie," she whispered, as though to herself.

A man who was likely a day laborer guided us halfway to our destination. Eikichi and I went on to an inn where, he said, the former district mayor was the innkeeper. We bathed, then ate a lunch of fresh fish.

"Please use this to buy some flowers for tomorrow's services." I gave Eikichi a small packet of money before he returned to his lodging house. I had to return to Tokyo on the morning boat the next day because I had no more money with which to travel. I told Eikichi that school was about to start, so I could not stay with them any longer.

I ate dinner less than three hours after lunch. Alone, I crossed the bridge to the north of Shimoda and climbed the hill Shimoda Fuji to view the harbor. When I called at Koshuya on my way back, the entertainers were eating a dinner of chicken stew.

"Won't you at least have a bite with us? It's not very appetizing now that we women have put in our chopsticks, but maybe this could be the makings of a funny story." The woman took a bowl and chopsticks out of the wicker basket and asked Yuriko to wash them.

They pleaded with me to delay my departure at least one more day, as tomorrow would be the forty-ninth day since the baby's death. But again I used school as an excuse and declined their invitation.

The woman spoke again. "Well, then, during winter vacation, we'll all come out to meet your boat. Just let us know what day you'll arrive. We'll be waiting. Now don't try staying at an inn or anything. We'll meet you at the boat."

When only Chiyoko and Yuriko were in the room, I invited them to a movie. Chiyoko held her stomach saying, "I don't feel well. I'm too weak to walk that far." She slumped down, her face pale. Yuriko stiffened and hung her head. The dancing girl was playing with the innkeeper's children on the stairs. When she heard me, she clung to the woman, begging for permission to go to a movie with me. She returned crestfallen. She set out my clogs.

"What do you mean? There's no harm in letting him take her by himself," Eikichi interjected. But the woman would not assent. I thought it indeed strange that she would not let us go together. As I went out the door, the dancing girl was stroking the puppy's head. The atmosphere was so restrained that I could not speak a word.

The dancing girl lacked the vitality even to lift her face and look at me.

I went to the movie alone. The woman narrator read the script of the silent movie by the light of a tiny lamp. I left as soon as it ended and returned to my inn. Resting my elbows on the windowsill, I stared out into the night town for a long time. It was a dark town. I thought I might hear a faint drum sounding far away. Inexplicably my tears fell.

7

While I was eating breakfast the next morning, Eikichi called to me from the street. He was wearing a crested black *haori*. Apparently, he had dressed formally to send me off. There was no sign of the women. I felt sad. Eikichi came up to my room.

"Everyone else wanted to come see you off, but they went to bed so late, they couldn't get up. They won't be coming. They said they'll be waiting for you this winter, so please do come."

The morning autumn breeze blew chill in the town. Along the way Eikichi bought four packs of Shikishima cigarettes, some persimmons, and a mouthwash called "Kaoru" for me. "Because my sister's name is Kaoru." He smiled faintly. "Mandarin oranges aren't the best thing to eat on a boat, but persimmons are good for seasickness, so you can have these."

"Here. You take this." I pulled off my hunting cap and placed it on Eikichi's head. Then I dug my school cap out of my bag, and we laughed as I smoothed the wrinkles.

As we approached the dock, I was struck by the sight of the dancing girl crouching near the water. She remained motionless until I reached her. Silently, she lowered her head. Her makeup, the same this morning as it was the previous night, made me feel even more sentimental. The rouge at the corners of her eyes bestowed a youthful strength, as though she might even be angry.

"Are the others coming?" Eikichi asked.

She shook her head.

"Are they still asleep?"

She nodded.

Eikichi went to buy my ticket for the boat to Tokyo and our passes for the launch. While he was gone, I tried to make small talk, but the dancing girl said nothing. She just stared down at the water pouring from a drainpipe into the sea. She just kept nodding over and over before I even finished speaking.

"Granny, this fellow looks nice." A man approached who looked like a laborer.

"You're a student, aren't you? Going back to Tokyo? I think I can trust you. Would you accompany this old lady to Tokyo? She's had some hard times. Her son was working at the silver mine at Rendaiji. But he and his wife both died in the flu epidemic. They left three children behind. We couldn't think of anything else to do, so we talked it over, and we're sending them back to their old hometown. That's Mito in Ibaraki Prefecture. But this old woman doesn't understand anything, so when the boat gets to Reiganjima in Tokyo, would you put her on a train to Ueno? I know it's a lot of trouble, but we're begging you. Just look at her. Don't you think it's pitiful?"

The old woman stood there with a blank expression,

an infant strapped to her back. Two girls, about three and five, held her hands. I could see big rice balls and pickled plums in her dirty bundle. Five or six miners were looking after the old woman. I was pleased to accept the task.

"Thank you. We're counting on you."

"Thank you. We really should see her all the way to Mito, but we can't." The miners expressed their gratitude.

The launch rocked violently. The dancing girl kept her mouth shut tight, staring at the same spot. When I grabbed the rope ladder and looked back, she tried to say good-bye but gave up and merely nodded one last time. The launch headed back to the wharf. Again and again Eikichi waved the hunting cap I had just given him. As the launch receded in the distance, the dancing girl began to wave something white.

The steamship left Shimoda. I leaned against the railing and gazed at Oshima in the offing until the southern tip of the Izu Peninsula vanished behind me. It already seemed long ago that I parted from the dancing girl. When I glanced into the cabin to check on the old woman, I saw a group of people gathered around her in a circle, consoling her. I felt relieved. I entered the cabin next door. The waves were choppy on Sagami Bay. I was tossed left and right as I sat. A crewman passed out small metal bowls. I lay down, using my bag as a pillow. My head felt empty, and I had no sense of time. My tears spilled onto my bag. My cheeks were so cold I turned my bag over. There was a boy lying next to me. He was the son of a factory owner in Kawazu and was on his way to Tokyo to prepare to enter school. The sight of me in my First Upper School cap seemed to elicit his goodwill.

After we talked for a while, he asked, "Have you had a death in your family?"

"No, I just left someone."

I spoke meekly. I did not mind that he had seen me crying. I was not thinking about anything. I simply felt as though I were sleeping quietly, soothed and contented.

I was not aware that darkness had settled on the ocean, but now lights glimmered on the shores of Ajiro and Atami. My skin was chilled and my stomach empty. The boy took out some sushi wrapped in bamboo leaves. I ate his food, forgetting it belonged to someone else. Then I nestled inside his school coat. I felt a lovely hollow sensation, as if I could accept any sort of kindness and it would be only right. It was utterly natural that I should accompany the old woman to Ueno Station early the next morning and buy her a ticket to Mito. Everything seemed to melt together into one.

The lamp in the cabin went out. The smell of the tide and the fresh fish loaded in the hold grew stronger. In the darkness, warmed by the boy beside me, I let my tears flow unrestrained. My head had become clear water, dripping away drop by drop. It was a sweet, pleasant feeling, as though nothing would remain.

DIARY OF MY SIXTEENTH YEAR

Author's note: What is written in brackets are explanations that I added when I was twenty-seven.

MAY 4

It was about five-thirty when I got home from middle school. The gate was closed to keep visitors away. My grandfather was sleeping alone in the house, so he would have been distressed if anyone came. [At the time, my grandfather was almost blind with cataracts.]

"I'm home," I called. But no one answered, and the house became quiet again. I felt the loneliness and sadness. About six feet from my grandfather's pillow, I called again:

"I'm home."

I got within three feet and called sharply:

"I just got home."

Then, five inches from his ear:

"I just now came home."

"Oh, you did. But I didn't have you here to help me pee since morning, so I've been lying here groaning, just waiting for you. I wanted to turn over to face west. That's why I was groaning. Will you turn me over to face west? All right?"

"Here, pull back."

"Oh, that's fine. Now put the quilt over me," my grandfather said.

"That's not right yet. One more time."

"That's [seven words here unclear]."

"Oh, this still isn't right. Let's do it over, okay?"

"Oh, that feels comfortable. You did a good job. Is the tea boiling? Later would you help me pee?"

"Just wait a minute. I can't do everything at once."

"I know, but I just wanted to remind you."

Then, a moment later:

"Come here." It was a lifeless voice that might have come from the mouth of a corpse.

"Would you help me pee? Help me."

He just lay motionless in bed, moaning. I did not know what to do.

"What should I do?"

"Bring the urinal and put my penis inside."

I had no choice; I uncovered him and did as he asked, though it disgusted me.

"Is it in? Okay? I'm going to pee now. Is it all right?" Couldn't he even feel his own body?

"Oh! Oh! It hurts. It hurts. It hurts! Oh! Oh!" He always has pain when he urinates. His labored breathing and fading voice—in the depths of the urinal, the sound of pure water in a valley stream.

"Oh! It hurts!" Tears welled up in my eyes as I listened to his voice. It seemed he could scarcely endure any more.

The tea was ready, so I had him drink some. Coarse tea. I held the cup to his mouth as he drank. His bony face, his balding, gray head. His quivering hands of skin and bone. His Adam's apple in a crane's neck that bobbed as he gulped. Three cups of tea.

"Oh, that was good. Good." He smacked his lips. "This is how I nurture my energy. You bought me that high-quality tea, but they say it's poison to drink too much of it. So I drink coarse tea."

A moment later:

"Did you send the postcard to Tsunoe?" [My grandfather's sister's village]

"Yes. I sent it this morning."

"Oh. You did."

Has Grandfather become aware of "that certain thing"? Has he somehow caught wind of it? [I was afraid that Grandfather had had me send a postcard to his younger sister, who never wrote, to encourage her to visit because he sensed his own approaching death.] I stared at my grandfather's pallid face until my eyes were blurry.

While I was reading, I heard someone approaching.

"Is it you, Omiyo?" my grandfather called.

"Yes."

"How did it go?"

A vast uneasiness filled my chest. I turned away from the table. [I had placed a table in the parlor. Omiyo was a farm woman about fifty years old. She came from her own home every morning and evening to cook and do other chores for us.]

"I went today. I told her that you were seventy-five years old and the reason why you are resting in bed. I said you had been eating well for a month, but without a bowel movement, so I wanted her to consult the god. She said, 'Age being what it is, nothing happens suddenly. It's old age.'"

They both heaved a great sigh. Omiyo kept on talking.

"She said, 'When you eat well and don't have a bowel movement, it means a creature in your belly is eating the food.' She didn't say anything like, 'Have him eat more than he has been. Get more down his throat than you have until now,' but she did say, 'The creature likes sake.' When I asked her what we should do, she said, 'Place a scroll of the Bodhisattva Myoken over the sick man, and burn some blessed incense throughout the room.' Even if you do have a creature in you, there hasn't been any particularly big change, except that you've lost your sense of time. Still, it used to be that even a single flake of dried fish would get stuck in your throat, but lately you can eat sushi or rice balls in a single bite. Oh, yes, and the way your Adam's apple bobs up and down makes me worry. When the Inari god occupies the medium and then when the god leaves her, her Adam's apple bobs, too. And on top of that, you drank an awful lot of sake a while back. I would guess what the medium said today was on the mark."

"Hmm."

I did not have the courage to tell them that it was all superstition. I was confused, overcome by a strange anxiety.

"Then I returned to my home and told them I had [gone] to Itsukaichi [the name of a village] to have the medium tell your fortune. They said, 'Did she say that he was going to die?' So I said no, that there wouldn't be anything sudden, that it was old age. She said it was a demon. I told them I had only gone to have your fortune told because you hadn't had a bowel movement in a month.

"Then as soon as I got here, I filled the room with incense smoke. I said, 'You [she meant the creature] should not be bothering an old established family like this. And besides, why would you cause a person such harm without any reason? If you want tea or food, just say so and we'll give you some. Hurry up and go. Go.' I thought I would reason with the creature. I thought it would be good to offer tea and rice to the northwest corner, starting tomorrow. And would you let me take one sword out of the storehouse to keep away demons? We'll take it out of its sheath and place it under the mats in the sleeping room. Then I'll go consult the Inari god once more tomorrow."

"That's so odd. I wonder if it's true."

"Well, I wonder if it is."

At my grandfather's pillow:

"Grandfather, a letter came from someone called Kano in Onobara [the name of a village]. Did you ever borrow money from him?"

"Yes, I did."

"When?"

"Seven or eight years ago."

"I see."

Another one has leapt out at me. [What I meant was that about that time, one by one, I kept discovering debts my grandfather had incurred here and there.]

"You just can't keep up with it all," Omiyo said. [I had consulted with Omiyo about the money.]

At supper my grandfather was eating seaweed-wrapped sushi. Oh! That! Would the creature be eating that? There, his Adam's apple moved. The food is really going into a human mouth. How foolish, how foolish to imagine . . . But, the words "a creature is eating" were carved into my head and would not leave. I took a sword out of the storehouse, waved it about over my grand-father's bedding, then put it underneath. Afterward, I thought it a bizarre act myself. But when Omiyo saw me cutting through the air in the room, she spoke very seriously.

"That's the way. That's the way." She stood there and encouraged me. How people would have laughed if they had seen me, thinking I was crazy.

"Omiyo. Omiyo."

It finally got dark. Occasionally, as I read, I could hear a frail voice send a shudder through the night air and the sound of Omiyo's footsteps each time as she went to help my grandfather relieve himself. Soon it seemed that Omiyo had gone home. I gave my grandfather tea to drink.

"Ah, yes. Good. Good." He gulped the tea, his Adam's apple bobbing up and down. I wondered if the creature was drinking this, too. That's stupid. Stupid. There couldn't be anything as weird as that. I'm a third-year middle-school student.

"Ah, that was good. Tea is fine, and it's good plain. It's bad for you to drink tea that tastes too good. Ah, this is fine. . . . Where's my tobacco?"

When I brought the lamp close to his face, he opened his eyes a bit. "What's that?" he said. Oh, those eyes that I thought would never see again—those eyes can see! I was happy; a gleam of light had pierced the dark world. [It is not that I had thought my grandfather's blindness would be cured. He probably had his eyes closed at the time. I must have been worried that he would die that way.]

■■■

As I have written up to this point, I have thought about a number of things. Brandishing the sword a while ago seems odd now. It seems foolish. But the words "a creature in his belly is eating and drinking" have taken hold of me.

It's about nine o'clock now. "He is possessed by a creature." The absurdity of the notion is gradually becoming more apparent. My brain feels as though it has been washed clean.

About ten o'clock, Omiyo came to help my grandfather urinate.

"I want to turn over. Which way am I facing now? Oh, I see. East?"

"Heave ho," Omiyo said.

"Ohhh."

"One more time," Omiyo said.

"Ohhh." His voice was wracked with pain. "Am I facing west now?"

"You go to sleep. I'm going home. There's nothing more to do now, is there?"

Soon Omiyo left.

MAY 5

Morning. As soon as the sparrows started chirping, Omiyo arrived.

"Really. Two times? You got up at twelve and three to help him pee? You're so young to have to go through so much. Think of it as repaying a debt of gratitude to your grandfather. We have a new baby at home, so I can't stay over here. Okiku knows what it is to give birth to a child, but she doesn't know what it is to care for one." [Okiku was Omiyo's daughter-in-law. She had just had her first baby at the time.]

"Think of it as repaying a debt of gratitude to your grandfather." These words satisfied me completely.

I went to school. School is my paradise. "School is my paradise"—Don't these words say everything about the situation in my home these days?

Omiyo came about six o'clock in the evening.

"I paid a visit to another shrine. The same thing happened. It's strange. She didn't say it was a creature, but a demon. She said, 'It's not just some creature without sense or reason, so you don't have to make too much of a fuss to get it out.' And on top of that, of course, she said he's just getting old. 'It won't happen suddenly, but gradually his body will get weaker.'"

"Gradually his body will get weaker."—I turned these words over several times in my chest.

"I see." I gave a sigh.

"And after that, what the Inari god said was right on the mark. The medium said, 'He's a little better these days, isn't he? He's probably not eating and drinking unreasonably.' You can see that too. He's quiet today."

I thought it strange that the Inari god should be able to guess the condition of a sick person. I began to puzzle again over whether there might really be such things as demons.

The smoke from the incense that we had bought with some of the little money in the house swirled around my grandfather's pillow and drifted over his bed like a brilliant, clear autumn stream.

"It's going to be hard when summer comes."

"Why?"

"We'll be busy with the fieldwork. I won't be able to come here. The way it looks now, I don't think he'll ever sit up by the charcoal brazier again."

As I continue to write, I wonder what will have become of my grandfather, my unfortunate grandfather, by the time I finish. [I had prepared a hundred sheets of manuscript paper and hoped to keep writing until I reached a hundred pages. I was worried that my grandfather might die before I reached a hundred. Perhaps I had believed my grandfather would be saved if only I could reach a hundred. And now that I suspected my grandfather might be dying, I wished at least to transfer his image to this diary while I still could.]

For a time my ailing grandfather's words became less contradictory. But, "a demon is cursing him"—was it a superstition? Or no superstition at all, but true?

MAY 6

"Has the boy gone to school yet?" my grandfather asked Omiyo.

"No. It's six in the evening now."

"Oh, I guess it is. Ha, ha, ha, ha, ha—." It was sad laughter.

For supper he had two thin rolls of seaweed-wrapped sushi. Omiyo put them in his mouth, and he swallowed them whole.

"Am I eating too much?" he asked her today. I listened from the bath. He did not normally ask such things.

Then, a moment later:

"It's still early, but I'm awfully hungry. Are you feeding me supper before the boy?"

"I think he just got out of the bath," Omiyo said.

"Maybe so."

I could not hear the rest, just that laughter again. I felt sad as I sat in the bath.

Night. The only sounds in the house are the tick of the wall clock and the jet of the gas lamps.

From the dark room in the back:

"It hurts. It hurts. Oh, it hurts." His voice spilled out in shreds. It sounded as though he was appealing to heaven. Finally, the voice stopped. Quiet. —Then again.

"Oooh. Ah, it hurts."

His short pained cries started and stopped and started and stopped until I went to bed.

As I listened, over and over I repeated the words in my heart, "It won't happen suddenly, but gradually his body will get weaker."

Still, my grandfather's head is clearer. He has his common sense back. He's more moderate about his eating.

Nevertheless, day by day, his body . . .

MAY 7

"Last night he woke me up once to help him pee and two other times to turn him over and to get him some tea. 'If you don't get up sooner, I'll run out of breath calling you.' He scolded me. But I had gone to bed at midnight, so I just didn't wake up."

I waited for Omiyo to come in this morning. I appealed to her.

"That's too bad. If my headache gets better, I'll stay here until midnight. Even in the daytime, if I don't come for two hours, when I do get here, he says, 'I have lived my life in tears,' so I've been coming every hour."

Last night I was sleepy, so when he woke me up and asked me all kinds of ridiculous, unreasonable things, I resented it and neglected him. Later I reconsidered what I had done and grieved and cried over my unfortunate grandfather.

When I was about to leave for school:

"I wonder when I'm going to get better?" my grandfather asked, in a voice that was nine parts despair clinging to one part hope.

"You'll get better when the weather settles down."

"I'm sorry I cause you so much trouble." It was a frail voice that begged pity. "I had a dream that the gods had gathered together over this house."

"It's good that you have faith in the gods."

"I could hear their voices. Isn't that a blessed occurrence? The gods and Buddhas won't abandon me. That's almost too good to be true." His voice was filled with satisfaction.

When I got home from school, the gate was open. But the house was silent.

"I'm home." I said it three times.

"Oh, is that you? Later on, would you help me pee?"

"Yes."

There is no task more odious to me than this. After

I ate, I turned back my grandfather's quilt, and held the urinal bottle. I waited ten minutes and nothing came. I realized how much strength had gone out of his belly. I complained while I waited. I grumbled. It should come out on its own. Then my grandfather begged my for-giveness. When I looked at his face, which grows more haggard day by day, his pale face where the shadow of death dwells, I was ashamed of myself.

Finally, "Oh, It hurts. It hurts. Oooh." His voice was frail and sharp. My shoulders grew tense just listening. Soon, the clear tinkling sound.

Night. When I rifled through the drawer in the table, I came across *A Theory of Safe House Construction*. It is a book that my grandfather dictated to Jiraku. [A man from a neighboring village, a disciple of my grandfather in the art of divining fortunes and the geomancy of house building. This was a book on the latter.] He tried to get it published and even consulted with Toyokawa [a rich man from Osaka], but nothing came of the manuscript. It lay hidden in the back of the drawer, completely forgotten. My grandfather never realized a single one of his life's ambitions. Everything he did was a failure. How does he feel in his heart? Oh, how well he has lived through adversity to the age of seventy-five. The strength of his heart. [I thought that the reason that my grandfather was able to live so long and endure such sorrow was because he had a strong heart.] He was completely alone, having had so many children and grandchildren die before him, with no one left to talk to, seeing and hearing nothing. [He was blind and hard of hearing.] The sorrow of loneliness—that is my grandfather. My grandfather's habit of saying "I have lived my life in tears" reveals his true feeling.

[My grandfather's divination and geomancy were quite accurate, so he was somewhat famous. There were even people who came from far away to have him check their plans. He probably thought that by publishing his *Theory of Safe House Construction* he would save people from the misfortunes of this world. It was not as though I believed or disbelieved his divination or geomancy. I recall that I had only a vague sense of what they were. Even so, no matter how far out in the country we lived, I can't believe that, being sixteen years old and a third-year middle-school student, I did not call a doctor to examine my grandfather, who had been constipated for a month. Instead, we had merely consulted a fortune teller at the Inari shrine and imagined he was possessed.]

[Also, it was through the business with the temple that my grandfather came to know the rich man Toyokawa. There was a convent temple in our village. Apparently my ancestors had founded the temple long ago. The temple buildings as well as the temple mountain, woods, and fields were in my family's name, and the nuns were listed in our family register. It was of the Obaku Sect, and the Bodhisattva Kokuzo was the principal image worshiped there. Once a year, on the "Thirteen Pilgrimage," the place was bustling with children who had turned thirteen. Anyway, a priest who had been secluded in a renowned mountain temple two and a half miles north of our village was to move to this temple. My grandfather was very grateful. He chased out the nuns and relinquished the temple property. The temple was rebuilt and enlarged, and its name changed. During the construction, the Kokuzo and five or six other Buddhist images were kept in the parlor of our house. Because of this, the house was filled with the green smell of the temporary reed mats that had been used because there was not enough money to install regular straw mats. The one who was so devoted to the new incoming priest, who rebuilt the temple, and who also laid mats in our parlor was the rich man Toyokawa.]

Occasionally I caught glimpses of my grandfather's gentleness. This morning Omiyo said, "I made rice cakes to celebrate the birth of the child, enough for thirty families. But we received gifts from more places than we ever expected, so I have to make some more."

"Really. Thirty houses' worth? More than that? In a village with fewer than fifty houses, a family like yours gets gifts from that many people?"

After that, he was crying for joy, tears choking his voice. [My grandfather was happy that a poor family of tenant farmers like Omiyo's should receive gifts from so many people.]

Omiyo felt sorry for me, having to care for my grandfather. About eight o'clock in the evening when she was about to leave, she said to my grandfather, "Do you need to pee?"

"No."

"Well, then, I'll be back again one more time later on."

I wanted to speak, but ended up saying nothing. "I'm here, so you don't need to come," I almost said.

MAY 8

This morning my grandfather looked forward to Omiyo's arrival. He reported my unkindness to her and complained endlessly. Maybe I was at fault. But I was angry at being awakened time after time in the night. And besides, I hate helping him urinate.

Omiyo spoke to me:

"All he does is complain. He thinks only of himself and not the least about the people who take care of him. Even though we care for him, knowing it's a fate we may all share."

This morning I even thought of abandoning him. I always ask him if there is anything he needs before I go to school in the morning, but today I left without saying a word. Of course, by the time I got home from school, I began to feel sorry for him.

Omiyo spoke to me:

"I told him about going to have his fortune told the other day. He said, 'Thank you for going for me. I vaguely remember eating everything in two bites. I seem to remember being able to drink a lot.'"

When I heard this, I recalled again the creature that ate and drank in his stomach.

After supper, my grandfather spoke:

"Omiyo, I am going to tell you what is on my mind— an intimate talk—so you can feel relieved."

"Feel relieved" sounded odd to me.

"As many troubles as we have, what are we supposed to feel relieved about?" Omiyo laughed.

"That's enough of that. Give me my supper."

"You just now ate."

"Oh. I didn't know. I forgot."

I was saddened and amazed. His words become quieter, more dejected, harder to catch as the days go by. He repeats the same things over and over, ten times or more.

Well, now I am sitting at my desk with my writing

paper spread out. Omiyo sat down and got ready to hear this so-called "intimate talk." [I was thinking I would take down my grandfather's words as I heard them.]

"You know about the boy's bank seal? That's right. While I am alive, I want to do something about that seal. [I don't know what he was talking about.] Oh, I've failed at everything and wasted the estate that was passed down from my ancestors. But, anyway, I gave it a try. I had wanted to go to Tokyo and meet Okuma [Okuma Shigenobu]. I have grown so weak sitting in this house. —Oh, we had over forty acres of fields and all I wanted to do was make them the boy's during my lifetime, but it amounted to nothing. [From the time he was young, my grandfather tried his hand at all kinds of things, like growing tea or manufacturing vegetable gelatin, but they all ended in failure. Then he would worry about the divination of the house. He would build and tear down and rebuild, selling off the fields and woods for a song. One part of the property he lost wound up in the hands of a sake brewer name Matsuo from Nada. My grandfather was always thinking that he would at least like to get back this part.] If I could just leave the boy thirty acres or so, he would be set. He wouldn't have to flounder about after he graduates from the university. It would be unfortunate if he has to depend on the Shimakis [my uncle's family] or the Ikedas [my aunt's family]. If those fields belonged to the boy, he could stay on in this house even after I die, consulting with Gozen [the monk who came to the new temple that I wrote about earlier]. If only I had money like a Konoike [a word that means "rich man"], he wouldn't have to hustle for a living. In order to bring this all about, you see, I had planned to go to Tokyo, but unfortunately I can't go. But words are not enough. If I hurried and made the boy the master of a solid family, he wouldn't need other people to take care of him the rest of his life. If I could see, I could go to Okuma and there would be no problem. Oh, no matter what, I'm going to Tokyo. I want you to talk with Jiko and Zuien [the new priest at the temple and his disciple] at Saihoji [our family temple], please. Tell them I'm going."

"If you did that you would be called the crazy man of Higashimura."

[My grandfather also had his own purpose in mind in wanting to go to Tokyo to see Okuma Shigenobu. My grandfather knew something about Chinese medicine. And my late father had been a doctor who had graduated from a medical school in Tokyo. My grandfather had picked up a few Western medical techniques and spiced the knowledge with his own version of Chinese pharmacology. He had been dispensing medicine to the country people for a long time, with an obstinate confidence in his self-taught expertise. This confidence grew even stronger when an outbreak of dysentery occurred in the village. It happened the summer of the year that the Buddhist images were left in our parlor during the reconstruction of the convent temple that I wrote of earlier. In our village of fifty houses, about one person per family was stricken with the disease, a large number of victims. It caused such a panic that they built temporary quarantine shelters in two places. The smell of disinfectants reached all the way out into the fields. Some villagers even said the disease was a curse for moving the old Buddhist images from the convent temple. Anyway, my grandfather's medicine cured some cases of dysentery quite readily. Some of the patients were saved by keeping them hidden at home, not letting them be taken to the hospital, and secretly giving them grandfather's medicine. There were even patients in the quarantine hospitals who tossed aside the prescribed medicine and took my grandfather's instead. My grandfather's medicine cured some people whom the doctors had given up for lost. I do not know what medical value it actually had, but my grandfather's treatment had indeed proven uncannily effective. Thereafter my grandfather began to consider making his medicine known to the world. He had Jiraku write a request by which he received permission from the Ministry of Home Affairs to sell three or four kinds of medicine. He printed up some five or six thousand wrapping papers with the shop name "Higashimura Sanryudo" on them, but ultimately his medicine production came to naught. Still, plans for that medicine remained in my grandfather's head until he died. My grandfather had a childlike confidence, certain that he could get the assistance he needed if only he could go to Tokyo and see Okuma Shigenobu, whom he esteemed so. Besides the medicine, he was probably also thinking about the publication of his book on safe house construction.]

"This family came into being in the time of Hojo Yasutoki and has lasted for seven hundred years, so it will continue on into the future as before. It will return to its old glory."

"You talk big. You sound as though it's going to happen at any moment." Omiyo laughed.

"In all my life, we never needed the help of Shimaki and Ikeda, but now . . . I never thought it would come to this. . . . When I think about it, Omiyo, it makes me sad. Listen to me. Consider these things I feel most deeply."

Omiyo found him hilarious; she had been convulsed with laughter for some time. I continued transcribing my grandfather's words.

"I'm at the point where I have only one breath left. My body has grown weak. If we had two or three thousand, we could manage, but one hundred twenty or thirty thousand. . . . Ah, I'm asking the impossible. Even if I couldn't go, if Okuma would come here. . . . Do you think that's funny? Please don't laugh like that. You shouldn't make fun of a person that way. I'll make the impossible possible. Right, Omiyo? If I can't make it possible, then a seven-hundred-year-old family will go to ruin."

"But even so, you have the boy. If you get yourself all worked up trying to pull a star out of the sky, you'll just make your illness worse."

"Am I a fool?" His voice was sharp. "If only I had life in me. . . . Oh, once in my life I want to see that old man [Okuma]. I can't keep backing up. Ah, even if I become a Buddha, I want to keep this feeling in my small chest. When you look at me, do you think I'm a fool? . . . Would you help me pee? . . . If it's all impossible, I might as well fall in a pond and die. Ah."

I grieved in my heart. I did not smile but made a pained expression as I copied down each word. Omiyo's laughing stopped. She listened, her cheek resting on her hand.

"I had first thought I'd go to Tokyo, and now I have ended up like this. Everything has gotten in the way. Hail Amida Buddha. Hail Amida Buddha. If it's all impossible, then I'd rather fall into a pond and die. I just don't have what it takes. Hail Amida Buddha. Hail Amida Buddha. Oh, to be laughed at when I have the courage to speak my heart. I don't want to live in a world like this. Hail Amida Buddha. Hail Amida Buddha."

The lamplight seemed to grow dimmer.

"Oh, oh." His suffering voice grew gradually louder.

"It's not right to live so long in this world only moving

backward. Men who have lived fifty years with a heart like mine are prime ministers. [At the time, Okuma Shigenobu was prime minister.] It's a shame I can't move. A shame."

Omiyo comforted my grandfather. "It's the misfortune we all have to deal with. But won't it be good if the boy makes his own way in the world?"

"Makes it? I know how far he'll go." He spoke loudly and glared at me. —What a doddering old fool he is.

"That may be true, but you needn't be jealous of people with a lot of money. Look at Matsuo. Look at Katayama. What counts is a person's character." [Both Matsuo, the sake brewer, and Katayama, a relative, had fallen on hard times.]

"Hail Amida Buddha."

My grandfather's long beard shone silver in the lamplight. He looked sad.

"I haven't the least attachment to this world. The other world is more important than this. But I don't want to go to paradise after having done nothing but backpedal my whole life."

"For the last while he's said he wanted the priest from Saihoji Temple to come because he had something to discuss with him. But they kept telling me the priest was out, so your grandfather was offended." Omiyo waited for a break in my grandfather's words and tried to explain my grandfather's ill temper to me. Indeed, I was offended, too. I sympathized with my grandfather. They don't need to put him off like that.

"In this world of people . . . not yet graduated from middle school . . . ah."

Today my grandfather despised me so.

Finally he turned over, facing away from me. I opened my textbook to study for my English examination tomorrow. My world has become hectic—rigid, as though I am being crammed up against four walls. My grandfather's voice tonight was not a voice of this world. After Omiyo went home, I kept thinking I would tell my grandfather about my hopes for the future and try to comfort him. The night grew late.

"The course of one's life is a difficult thing." My grandfather suddenly spoke, as if from the depths.

"Yes. It's difficult," I said.

MAY 10

This happened in the morning:

"Hasn't the chief priest from the temple come yet?" my grandfather asked.

"No, he hasn't," I said.

"Jiraku hasn't come at all lately. He was coming every day, wasn't he? I want to have him read my face once and tell my fortune."

"Your face hasn't changed since the last time. It can't change that fast."

"I won't rest easy until I consult the priest. Once I've had my face read, I'll know what I have to do."

His resolve manifested itself in his firm tone of voice.

"I want to see Jiraku."

"What good is a man like Jiraku going to be?" I whispered, as if to myself.

MAY 14

"Omiyo. Omiyo. Omiyo." I woke up at the sound of my grandfather's voice.

"What is it?" I got up.

"Has Omiyo come?"

"Not yet. It's about two o'clock in the morning."

"Oh, I see."

From then on until morning, my grandfather kept calling for Omiyo every five minutes. I listened to him as I drifted in and out of sleep. Omiyo came about five o'clock.

When I got home from school, Omiyo spoke to me:

"All he did was demand things all day long. I couldn't leave his side for a moment. 'Help me urinate.' 'Turn me over.' 'Give me some tea.' 'Get me some tobacco.' I haven't been able to go back home once since I got here this morning."

"Maybe I should call the doctor."

I have been thinking this for some time. But it takes money to call a good doctor. And since my grandfather does not think much of doctors, I worry that a doctor's examination would provoke him. And I wouldn't know what to do if he were to insult the doctor to his face.

And this morning:

"A doctor—he wouldn't be as useful as a nail clipper."

Night:

"Omiyo. Omiyo. Omiyo."

I purposely ignored his cries as I got close to his ear.

"What is it?"

"Is Omiyo gone? She didn't even feed me breakfast."

"Didn't you just eat supper? It hasn't even been an hour yet."

His countenance looked dull. I couldn't tell whether he had understood me or not.

"Turn me over."

He complained to me, but I didn't understand a thing he said. I asked him over and over again, but he didn't respond at all.

"Would you give me some tea? . . . Ah, this tea is just lukewarm. Oh, it's cold. This tea isn't any good." His voice was loathsome.

"Do whatever you like." I left his side without further word.

Then a little later.

"Omiyo. Omiyo."

He never called my name anymore.

"What is it?"

"Did you go to Ikeda [about thirteen or fourteen miles from my aunt's house] and see Eikichi?"

"I didn't go anyplace like Ikeda."

"Oh, then where did you go?"

"I didn't go anywhere."

"That's strange."

I was the one who felt strange, wondering what made him ask such a thing. Then when I was writing an essay for my homework, he called out again.

"Omiyo. Omiyo. Omiyo." His voice grew higher. It sounded as though he was having trouble breathing.

"What is it?"

"Help me urinate."

"All right. Omiyo isn't here now. It's past ten o'clock at night."

"Would you feed me something?"

I was dumbfounded.

My grandfather's legs and head are full of wrinkles like an old worn-out silk kimono. If you pinch up his skin, it stays that way and does not go back. I was forlorn. All he did all day was say things that hurt my feelings. Every time, my grandfather's face began to look more and more uncanny. Until I fell asleep, my head was filled with an unpleasant sensation because of my grandfather's sporadic moaning.

MAY 15

For the next four or five days Omiyo has some other business to attend to, so Otsune [the old woman who lives in the house by the village entrance] is coming in her place. When I got home from school, I spoke to Otsune.

"Otsune, he probably asked unreasonable things, didn't he?"

"No. Not at all. When I asked if there was anything I could do, he said he needed to urinate, but he was very quiet."

I thought his reserve was very touching.

He seemed to be in great pain today. I tried to comfort him, but the only sound he made was "oh, oh" over and over. I could not tell if it was an answer or a moan. His painful groaning echoed deep in my head. It made me feel as though my life were being cut away bit by bit.

"Oh, oh. Omiyo, Omiyo, Omiyo, Omiyo. Oh. Ah, ah."

"What is it?"

"I'm going to urinate. Hurry, hurry."

"It's all right, I'll catch it."

I waited five minutes holding the urinal bottle in place.

"Hurry and get the bottle."

He did not have any sensation. I was sad and pitied him.

He had a fever today. That disagreeable odor drifted

in the air. —I read a book at my desk. The long, high sound of his moaning. Early summer rain falling tonight.

MAY 16

About five o'clock in the evening, Shirobei [an old man in a branch family. I say branch family, but that is only on official records. He was not a blood relative, so my grandfather did not have any close dealings with him.] came to call on my grandfather. He said things to comfort my grandfather, whose only response was to groan. Shirobei gave me a lot of advice.

Then he left. "You're so young to have it so tough."

After seven o'clock:

"I'm going out to play." I dashed out of the house. About ten o'clock I came back. I reached the gate.

"Otsune. Otsune." I could hear my grandfather calling, his voice almost unable to bear the strain.

I hurried in. "What is it?"

"Where's Otsune?"

"She's already gone home. It's ten o'clock."

"Did Otsune feed you your dinner?"

"Yes, I ate."

"I'm hungry. Would you get me something to eat?"

"There isn't any food."

"Really. Well, what am I going to do?"

Our conversation was not really this orderly. He always repeats the same absurd things over and over. He says he heard what I said. Then he forgets right away and asks me the same thing again. I wonder what is wrong with his head.

1914

Afterword

This is the end of the diary. Ten years after I wrote it, this is what I found in my uncle Shimaki's storeroom. It was written on about thirty sheets of middle-school writing paper. That is probably all I wrote. I likely could not keep writing after that because my grandfather died the night of May 24. The last day covered in the diary is May 16, eight days before his death. After the sixteenth my grandfather's illness grew worse, and the house was in turmoil; it was no place to be writing in a diary.

What seemed strangest to me when I found this diary was that I have no recollection of the day-to-day life it describes. If I do not recall them, where have those days gone? Where had they vanished to? I pondered the things that human beings lose to the past.

Nevertheless, these days were kept alive in a leather bag in my uncle's storeroom, and now they have been resurrected in my memory. The bag was one my father, a doctor, had carried with him on house calls. My uncle recently went bankrupt due to a market failure and even lost his house. Before the storeroom was turned over to someone else, I searched through it in case something of mine had been kept there. That is when I discovered this old locked bag. When I cut the leather with a knife that was lying beside it, I found it full of journals from my youth. Among them was this diary. I came face-to-face with the emotions of my forgotten past. But the image of my grandfather here was much uglier than the one in my memory. Memory had purified my grandfather's image over the last ten years.

I could not recall the days in this diary, but naturally I remembered when the doctor first came and the day my grandfather died. Although my grandfather had always harbored an extreme contempt and mistrust of doctors, when he finally faced this one, he gave himself up to his care and thanked him, tears flowing from his eyes. Rather, it was I who felt as though I had been betrayed by my grandfather. I pitied him in such a state. It was painful to watch. My grandfather died on the evening of the great funeral for the widow of Emperor Meiji. I was torn as to whether I should attend the local memorial service. My middle school was in town, almost four miles south of my village. For some reason I felt anxious and wanted desperately to attend the ceremony. But would my grandfather die while I was gone?

Omiyo asked my grandfather about it.

"It's the responsibility of a Japanese citizen, so go ahead and go," Omiyo said.

"Will he stay alive until I get back?"

"Yes, he will. Go on."

Worried I might be late for the ceremony, I hurried along the road. One of the straps on my clogs broke. [At that time we wore Japanese clothing at my school.] I returned home dejected. Surprisingly, Omiyo said it was just an old superstition that a broken clog strap meant bad luck. She encouraged me to change clogs and hurry straight to the school.

When the ceremony was over, I grew uneasy. I recall that the lanterns lighted for the memorial service and hanging from the houses in the town were bright, so it must have been after nightfall. I took off my clogs and ran barefoot the whole way home. My grandfather lived until past midnight that night.

In August of the year my grandfather died, I left that house and was taken in by my uncle. When I thought of how attached my grandfather was to the house, it pained me then, as it did later when I sold the property. Then, as I drifted from relatives' houses to dormitories to lodging houses, the concepts of house and household were driven from my mind. All I saw were dreams of myself as a wanderer. My family's ancestral pedigree chart, which my grandfather hesitated to show to relatives was left in the care of Omiyo's family, whom my grandfather trusted most. To this day the record has been kept locked in a drawer in Omiyo's Buddhist family altar, but I have never wanted to see it. Still, I feel no particular guilt toward my grandfather for my lack of interest. That is because I believe, however vaguely, in the wisdom and benevolence of the dead.

Published in
Bungei Shunju
August, September 1925

Afterword II

"Diary of My Sixteenth Year" was published in 1925 when I was twenty-seven, but the diary from 1914, my sixteenth year, is the oldest piece of writing that I have published, so I have included it in the first volume of my complete works. ["Sixteenth year" refers to the old way of counting calendar years. I was actually fourteen years old.]

I added an afterword when I published it, and most of what I want to say about this diary I wrote in that afterword. But since I wrote that afterword as fiction, there are some parts that differ from the truth. I wrote, "My uncle recently went bankrupt due to a market failure and even lost his house." But the one who sold the house was my cousin. I think it was after my uncle had died. My uncle was a steady, cautious man. Also, the part about my father's medical bag being full of diaries from my early years was an exaggeration. I still have most of the diaries from my middle-school years, and there are not that many.

I recall the bag my father used for house calls, but it was not the kind of bag that the average doctor of his time carried. It had a wide bottom like a traveling bag. Now I am not quite clear about the number of pages, although I wrote, "It was written on about thirty sheets of middle-school writing paper." After I copied it at the age of twenty-seven, I tore up the original and threw it away.

Anyway, when I got out all my old diaries in the process of editing my complete works, I found two pages that were entitled "Diary of My Sixteenth Year." They are the twenty-first and twenty-second pages. When I recopied the diary at the age of twenty-seven, these two pages got separated and I failed to copy them, so I never tore them up. Because I did not write just one character in each box on the manuscript paper—there were twenty-one lines with twenty spaces in each—actually far more characters were written there, so perhaps I estimated the diary to be thirty pages.

These two pages should have been included in "Diary of My Sixteenth Year" but were left out. There was no date on them, but they are certainly a continuation, so I have decided to copy them here. Then I will tear up these two pages as well and throw them away.

"I don't feel well. Oh, people die who shouldn't." I could barely catch what he said in his extremely low voice.

"Someone died?"

" . . . [unclear] . . . "

"Do you mean yourself?"

"Everyone in the world dies."

"What?"

These words would not seem strange at all if you were to hear them from the average person. But my heart would not allow these words from my grandfather to pass without consideration. I made all kinds of associations. I was seized by a certain anxiety. [five words unclear]

My grandfather's moaning continues in intervals, short and weak. It seems as though he only expels his breath in short bursts. His condition is taking a turn for the worse.

"Omiyo? What's become of me? —Morning, night, lunch, supper, I have lived as though in a dream. Oh, I hate being nursed: 'If you just feed him it will be okay.' —After I heard the talk about the gods the other day, it weighed on my mind, it just weighed on my mind. Have the gods and Buddhas given me up?"

"It's not like that. The gods will take good care of you," Omiyo said.

My grandfather spoke from the depths of a cavity, complaining. "Oh, I used it for nothing for a year [he used the loan for a year without paying interest]. I worried and fretted about a mere ten *ryo*." He repeated the same thing more than ten times. As he spoke, his breathing became gradually more labored.

"Why don't we have a doctor take a look at you?" Omiyo suggested. All I could do was nod in agreement.

"Grandfather, why don't we have a doctor look at you? It would be unfortunate for your family if you got worse." [I did not record how my grandfather responded. Though I had expected him to refuse, he surprised me by meekly consenting. So I recall it made me feel rather sad.]

We had the old woman Otsune run to the doctor at Yadogawara.

While she was gone, Omiyo spoke to my grandfather.

"My children and I have already received the money from Sanban [the name of my uncle's village] and borrowed the part for Kobata from Tsunoe [my grandfather's younger sister's village] and paid it, so don't worry."

"Really. That makes me happy."

This was true joy for my grandfather in the midst of his suffering.

"You feel relieved now. You should chant a prayer to Buddha."

"Hail, Amida Buddha. Hail, Amida Buddha."

Oh, my grandfather's life won't last much longer. He probably won't last long enough for me to finish. [I had prepared one hundred sheets of manuscript paper.] My grandfather has weakened visibly in the few days that Omiyo has been gone. Now the mark of death is on him.

I put down my pen, and in a daze I thought about what would happen after my grandfather's death. Oh, my grievous self, I will be alone in heaven and earth.

My grandfather continued his chanting.

"Hearing that, my belly is all relaxed. Until now it was tense."

Otsune came back. She said the doctor was out.

"He'll be coming back from Osaka tomorrow, but if that's not soon enough, we can ask somewhere else."

"What shall we do?" Omiyo said.

"Well, it's not that pressing," Otsune said.

"No, I don't think there's anything that pressing," I said; nevertheless, my heart raced when I heard the doctor was away.

My grandfather is already snoring. I suppose he is

asleep. His mouth is open. He is a hollow figure, his eyes half-open.

In the dim light of the oil lamp beside his pillow, the two women sat, silently resting their cheeks in their hands.

"Well, boy, what shall we do? —Even with his condition this bad, he still complains."

"I wonder myself." I felt I was about to cry.

The original manuscript was one and a half pages plus three lines, but once I had copied it, it came to four pages and four lines. The only thing that I am certain of about this manuscript is that it comes after the portion that I had published when I was twenty-seven. "Diary of My Sixteenth Year" ends with the record of the sixteenth, the day after Omiyo went home because of something she had to do, and the old woman Otsune came in her place, but the part I have copied here is from later on, when Omiyo came to our house again.

Therefore, the statement in the afterword of "Diary of My Sixteenth Year," "This is the end of the diary," is not true. I had found only the portion up to the sixteenth of May when I published "Diary of My Sixteenth Year." I am inclined to think that there may have been several more entries between the sixteenth and the portion I have copied here. Perhaps I lost them.

My grandfather died on May 24, so the sixteenth was eight days before he died. What I have copied here was written a few days closer to my grandfather's death.

The death of my grandfather, when I was sixteen, left me with no close living relatives and no house.

I wrote in the afterword, "What seemed strangest to

me when I found this diary was that I have no recollection of the day-to-day life it describes. If I do not recall
them, where have those days gone? Where had they
vanished to? I pondered the things that human beings
lose to the past." The mystery of having experienced
something in the past but not remembering it is still a
mystery to me now at the age of fifty. To me, this is the
main problem of "Diary of My Sixteenth Year."

I cannot simply imagine that something has "vanished" or "been lost" in the past just because I do not
recall it. This work was not meant to resolve the puzzle
of forgetfulness and memory. Neither was it intended to
answer the questions of time and life. But it is certain
that it offers a clue, some piece of evidence.

My memory is so bad that I can have no firm belief
in memory. There are times I feel that forgetfulness is a
blessing.

The second problem is why I wrote a diary like this.
Sensing that my grandfather was near death, I must have
wanted to describe him while I still could. Imagining
myself at sixteen, sitting beside my dying grandfather
and writing in my diary as if sketching from nature—it
is quite strange.

In the entry for May 8 it reads, "Well, now I am sitting at my desk with my writing paper spread out. Omiyo
sat down and got ready to hear this so-called 'intimate
talk.' [I was thinking I would take down my grandfather's words as I heard them.]" It says "desk"; however,
I remember it more like this: "I placed a candle on the
edge of the footstool I was using as a desk and wrote
'Diary of My Sixteenth Year' on it." My grandfather was
nearly blind, so he would not have noticed that I was
writing about him.

Of course I never dreamed that ten years later I

would be publishing this diary as a work of literature. Nevertheless, the fact that one is able to read it as a work of literature is thanks to my verbal sketches. I was not a young literary genius. In order to take down my grandfather's words, I kept scribbling as though taking shorthand, with no time to embellish the lines. There were passages I could not decipher later.

My grandfather died at the age of seventy-five.

OIL

My father died when I was three, and my mother died the following year, so I do not remember a single thing about my parents. Not even a photograph remains of my mother. My father was a handsome man, so perhaps he enjoyed having his picture taken. I found thirty or forty photographs of my father at various ages in the storage room when we sold my family's old home. I kept the best-looking one on my desk while I was living in a dormitory during middle school. Eventually, however, as I changed my lodgings time and again, I lost every last photograph. Seeing his picture brought back no memories. And so, although I might imagine that the photographs were of my own father, the idea was not accompanied by a gut feeling. Everyone told me stories about my parents, but it was not like hearing gossip about someone familiar. I soon forgot them.

One New Year's, as I was about to cross Sori Bridge on my way to pay my respects at Sumiyoshi Shrine in Osaka, a vague sensation arose, as though I had once crossed this bridge when I was a child. I spoke to my cousin, who was with me.

"I wonder if I once crossed this bridge when I was a

small child. Somehow I feel as though I did."

"Well, you may have. When your father was alive, you were nearby, in Sakai and Hamadera. He surely would have brought you here," she said.

"No, it seems as though I crossed it alone."

"But that would have been impossible. A child of three or four couldn't have crossed this bridge alone. It's too dangerous. Your mother or father probably carried you."

"Perhaps. But it seems I crossed it by myself."

"You were a child when your father died. You were so excited to have the house bustling with funeral guests. Still, you hated it when the nails were hammered into the coffin. You weren't going to let them drive the nails. Nobody knew what to do with you."

When I came to Tokyo to enter high school, my aunt, whom I had not seen for over ten years, was amazed to see me as an adult.

"Children grow up, even without parents. How happy your father and mother would be if they were still alive. When your father died and then again when your mother died, you were so unreasonable, I didn't know what to do. You hated the sound of the bell that is struck before the Buddhist altar. You cried and fussed so much when you heard the sound that we decided not to strike it. On top of that, you told me to put out the lights in the altar. You not only told me to put them out, you broke the candles and poured the oil from the clay altar vessel into the garden. You refused to control your temper. At your father's funeral your mother was so angry she cried."

I do not remember any of it—what I heard from my cousin about how happy I was that the house was bustling with guests at my father's funeral or that I tried to stop them from driving nails into my father's coffin. However, in my aunt's words, I discovered the sort of intimacy one feels when one has been visited by a long-lost friend from childhood. My own face as a child came to mind—crying as I held the clay vessel, my hands smeared with oil. The moment I heard my aunt's story, I could picture in my heart the ancient tree in the garden of my old home. Until I was sixteen or seventeen, I climbed that tree every day and sat on a limb like a monkey, reading books.

The spot where I poured out the oil was beside the washbasin in the garden, by the parlor veranda which faced that tree. I even recall such details. But, when I think about it, the place where my father and mother died was the house by the banks of the Yodo River near Osaka. What I picture in my mind now is the veranda of the house in a mountain village ten or twelve miles north. We tore down the house by the Yodo River shortly after my father and mother died, then moved to the old family home. I remember nothing of the house near the riverbank, so I imagined it was the house in the mountain village where I poured out the oil. The place would not necessarily have been near a stone washbasin, and it would have been more likely for my mother or grandmother to have been holding the clay vessel. Also, I can only recall the two events—my mother's death and my father's—as one incident or as a repetition of the same event. Even my aunt has forgotten the details. What I believe to be memories are probably daydreams. Still, my own sentimentality yearns for them as if they were the truth, suspect or twisted though they may be. I have forgotten that they were stories I heard from another and feel an intimacy with them as if they were my own direct memories.

My aunt's story worked a strange effect on me, as though it had a life in itself.

Three or four years after my parents died, when my grandmother died, and again three or four years after that when my older sister died, and again the many other times when my grandfather made me pray before the family Buddhist altar, he had a custom of always transferring the light from the oil lamp to the candles. Until I heard my aunt's story, I was never suspicious of why my grandfather did that. It simply lingered as a memory. It was not that I had an inborn hatred of oil lights or the sound of a bell. At my grandmother's and my sister's funerals, perhaps I was unconcerned about the light from the oil lamp, having forgotten that I had made someone pour out the oil at my parents' funerals. But my grandfather did not make me pray before the light of an oil lamp. When I heard my aunt's story, I was able to realize, for the first time, my grandfather's grief, which was contained within the story. Funny as it may seem, even though, according to my aunt, I broke the candles and poured out the oil at my parents' funerals, my grandfather transferred the light to candles. I vaguely recall pouring out the oil, but I cannot remember breaking the candles at all. The part about the candles was probably my aunt's faulty memory or her exaggeration for the sake of the story. Indeed, it was the light of the oil lamp of the family altar that my grandfather did not let me see; however, until I entered middle school, the two of us lived by the light of oil lamps. My grandfather was half-blind, so it made little difference to him whether it was light or dark. We used old-style lamps in place of kerosene lanterns.

Besides inheriting my father's weak constitution, I was also born a month prematurely. I looked as though

I had little hope of growing. Until I started elementary school, I would not eat rice. I hated many foods, but the one I despised the most was rapeseed oil. If I put anything in my mouth that smelled of rapeseed oil, I would invariably vomit. When I was little, I was quite fond of both fried eggs and rolled omelettes, but if I suspected the pan had been oiled with rapeseed oil, I was repulsed, even if I could not detect it. I would eat the eggs only after my grandmother or the maid peeled off the surface that had touched the pan. They repeated this troublesome procedure daily because of my poor appetite. Once, when a drop of oil from the lamp soaked into my kimono, they could not convince me to wear it again. Only after I made them cut out the spot and patch it could I pass my hand over it, though uneasily. To this day, I have been extremely sensitive to the smell of oil. I simply believed I hated the smell. But when I heard my aunt's explanation, I realized, for the first time, that my own grief was contained within the story. For me, who hated the oil light of the altar, perhaps my parents' deaths had permeated my heart like the smell of the oil. And also I could imagine, from my aunt's story, the feelings of my grandfather and grandmother as they forgave my willful hatred of oil.

When all this dawned on me after listening to my aunt, a dream I'd had crept up from the depths of my memory. There were many clay lamps, each burning, hanging in a line in midair like the hundred lanterns I had seen at a mountain shrine festival when I was a child. A fencing teacher—the scoundrel—led me before the lights and spoke.

"If you can break these clay vessels exactly in half with a bamboo sword, your arm is sufficiently skilled, and I shall bestow upon you the secrets of fencing."

Because I had nothing to use but a thick bamboo sword to knock down these unglazed vessels, they crumbled to dust. They would not break cleanly in two. I smashed them all, never looking aside, and when I came to my senses, every light was out. It was dark all around me. In other words, the swordsman had thus shown what a rascal he was, and I fled. Then I woke up.

I had dreamed a dream like this a number of times. When I consider it in connection with my aunt's story, I realize that the pain of having lost my parents as a child lurked within me, and that this dream was the manifestation of something inside me that still battled against that pain.

The moment I heard my aunt's story, I felt all the unconnected events I had stored in my memory converge on one spot, greeting one another and conversing about their common background. I felt my heart lighten. I wanted to reconsider the effects of losing my parents when I was a child.

When I was a youth, I grieved over my "orphan's sorrow" with sweet tears, just as I had placed my father's photographs on my desk. I appealed to the sympathy of my male and female friends.

But soon my reflections led me to realize that I understood nothing about an "orphan's sorrow" and that there was no way for me to understand. An orphan's sorrow is indeed knowing these two things: It would have been that way if they had lived, and it has turned out this way because they died. But because they are truly dead, only God knows how it would have been had they lived. It's not necessarily true that there would have been no sadness. And so the tears I shed for the deaths of parents whose faces I do not even know were born of a game of childish sentimentality. Certainly their deaths wounded me. But this wound would only be clear to me after I grew old and looked back on my life. I imagined that until then I would simply grieve according to emotional convention or after the form I had seen in literature.

My heart was braced and ready.

But after my life began to grow more relaxed and free in my high-school dormitory, I finally realized instead that it was my willfulness that had warped me. My feelings had worked to indulge my wounds and my weakness. I had meekly grieved for what I should grieve and sorrowed for that for which I should feel sorrow, and through that meekness I had prevented myself from healing my grief and sorrow. Long ago my life occasionally turned pitch black when I recognized the feelings and actions for which I should feel shame, which were clearly a result of having not received the love of parents since my childhood. Whenever that happened, I tended quietly to pity myself.

Seeing happy families at the theater or a park or other places, or seeing children playing together, I found myself charmed; and discovering that I was charmed, I felt touched; and discovering that I was touched, I scolded myself for being a fool. But now I think I was wrong.

Just as I lost all thirty or forty photographs of my father, I should not concern myself with my dead parents. I should not dwell on the orphan's spirit in me. "I have a truly beautiful spirit."

These are the feelings I had as I stepped out into the bright, open plaza of human life at the age of twenty. I came to feel that I was approaching happiness. Even the slightest good fortune began to make me giddy.

"Is this all I need?"

"Since I did not spend my childhood as a child should, it is all right to rejoice now like a child."

Thus I answered my own question and indulged myself to see myself anew. I even believed this single, wonderful happiness to come would cleanse me of my orphan's complex. I was impatient to see my new life then, like a person who has escaped a long stay in the hospital and sees the green of the fields for the first time.

The story my aunt told me had come to life inside me and transformed my feelings. I was struck by the sensation that I had been saved from one of the pains that my parents' deaths had caused me. I made up my mind to try eating some food that smelled of rapeseed oil. And strangely, I was able to eat it. I bought some rapeseed oil, put some on my finger, and tasted it. My nose was sensitive to the smell, but it did not bother me.

"This is it! This is it!" I cried.

There are many ways to interpret this transformation. You might even say that it was nothing at all; my voice rejoicing over having been saved won out, even though my inborn dislike of oil had nothing to do with my parents' deaths. But I also wish to say, however unreasonably, that, although I had forgotten the cause-and-effect relationship between my grief for my parents' deaths, which dwelt in the lights in the Buddhist altar, and my coming to hate the oil in those lights, my throwing the oil out in the garden—I wish to say that my hatred of oil was due to the accidental binding of cause and result from stories about my parents.

"You have been saved only from the oil." I want to believe this as proof that truly I had healed one of my wounds.

I also imagine that there is no way that the effect on me of losing my close relatives when I was a child will vanish until I become someone's husband and someone's father, until I am surrounded by blood relatives. But

I hope that, as with the oil, chance incidents can continue to save me a second or third time from the warped aspects of my heart.

More and more the desire stirs within me to have normal health, live long, develop my spirit, and accomplish my life's work. Excited about the oil, I smiled, thinking I should take cod liver oil for my health and that I could now swallow such a smelly, oily substance every day. Moreover, I even felt as though I would be adding reverence for my dead parents to my body every time I took it.

It has been almost ten years since my grandfather, also, died.

"The light is brighter now, isn't it?"

So saying, I want to offer a hundred oil lights on the altar for my parents.

July 1927

THE MASTER OF FUNERALS

1

Since I was a boy, I have had neither my own house nor home. During school vacations I stayed with relatives. I made the rounds of my many relatives from one house to another. However, I spent most of my school vacations at the homes of two of my closest relatives. These two houses were south and north of the Yodo River, one in a town in Kawachi Province and the other in a mountain village in Settsu Province. I traveled back and forth by ferry. At either house I was greeted not with "Thank you for coming" but with "Welcome home."

During the summer holiday when I was twenty-two, I attended three funerals in the space of less than a month. Each time, I wore my late father's silk gauze jacket, long divided skirts, and white socks, and I carried a Buddhist rosary.

First there was a funeral in a branch of the Kawachi household. The mother of the family's patriarch had died. She was quite old; they said she had grandchildren in their thirties and that she had been nursed through a long illness. You might say she had gone on to her reward without regrets. When I gazed at the patriarch's despondent appearance and the granddaughters' red eyes, I could see their grief. But my heart did not mourn directly for the late woman; I could not grieve her death. Although I burned incense before the altar, I did not know the face of the woman in the coffin. I had forgotten there even was such a person.

Before the coffin was carried out, I made a condolence call in mourning clothes, rosary and fan in hand, with my elder cousin who had come from Settsu. Compared to my cousin's behavior, what little I did, though I was young, appeared considerably more composed and appropriate for a funeral ceremony. I was comfortable performing my role. Surprised, my cousin studied my bearing and imitated me. Five or six cousins were gathered in the main house. They felt no need to make solemn faces.

About a week later, I was in Kawachi when I received a telephone call from my elder cousin in Settsu. There was going to be a funeral in a branch of the family into which his elder sister had married. You have to go, too, he told me. Previously, it seems, someone from that family had attended a funeral in my own. I took my cousin from Settsu as a companion and went by train. When we went to the house to offer our sympathy, I could not begin to guess which of the people there were family, except for the chief mourner. I did not even know who had died. My cousin's sister's house was the resting place for those attending, but her husband's family was in a separate room. In the room where I was, no one talked about the person who had died. All they did was worry about the heat and when the coffin would be removed.

Occasionally, a question arose—who died, or how old was the deceased? I played go as I waited for the coffin to be brought out.

Later that month, my cousin from Settsu called again from his work. He asked me to go in his stead to the funeral of a distant relative of the family of his elder sister's husband. My cousin didn't even know the family that was holding the funeral, the name of the village, or the location of the cemetery. While we were talking, my cousin joked, "I'm asking you because you're the master of funerals."

I was struck dumb. We were on the telephone, so my cousin couldn't see the expression on my face. I assented to this third funeral. My cousin's young wife at the Kawachi house where I received the call smiled wryly. "It's as though you're a funeral director." She gazed at my face as she continued sewing. Deciding to stay at the house in Settsu that night and then leave from there the next morning for the funeral, I crossed the Yodo River.

Hearing my cousin laughingly call me "the master of funerals" prompted me to reflect. My past had made me particularly sensitive to such words. It is true that since childhood I have attended more funerals than I can count; not only have I met with the deaths of my closest relatives, but I have also often represented my family in the country villages where everyone diligently attends each other's funerals.

I have learned the funeral customs of Settsu Province. I am most familiar with funerals of the Pure Land and New Pure Land sects of Buddhism, but I have also attended Zen and Nichiren funerals. I have witnessed the last moments of five or six people that I can remember. I can also recall three or four times when I moistened the lips of the dead with the last water. I have lighted the first incense and have also lighted the last so-called departing incense. I have participated in several ceremonies where ashes were gathered and placed in an urn. And I am well acquainted with the customs of Buddhist rites for the forty-ninth day after death.

I had never even met the three people whose funerals I attended that summer. There was no way I could feel any personal grief. But at the cemetery, when the incense was burned, I rid myself of worldly thoughts and quietly prayed for the repose of the dead. Although I noted that most of the young people present bowed their heads while leaving their hands to dangle at their sides, I pressed my palms together. People often assumed I was more genuinely pious than the others who had little relationship to the deceased. The reason I gave this impression was that funerals often inspired me to consider the lives and the deaths of people who were close to me. And, in the repose of contemplation, my heart grew still. The more distant my connection with the deceased, the more I felt moved to go to the cemetery, accompanied by my own memories, to burn incense and press my palms together in devotion to those memories. So it was that as a youth, my decorous behavior at the funerals of strangers was never feigned; rather, it was a manifestation of the capacity for sadness I had within myself.

2

I have no recollection of my parents' funerals. And I remember nothing about them when they were alive. People tell me, "Don't forget your parents. Always remember them." But I cannot, try though I might.

When I see a photograph, it strikes me as neither a drawing nor a living being. It is something in-between. Neither a relative nor a stranger, but something in-between. I feel a weird, awkward tension, as though the photograph and I are embarrassed to be facing each other. When anyone talks of my parents, I never know what sort of manner to adopt in listening. My only desire is that they finish quickly. When I am told the dates of their deaths or their ages at death, I immediately forget them, as if they were just random numbers.

I heard from my aunt that I cried and fussed on the day of my father's funeral. I told them, "Don't strike the bell on the altar," "Put out the light," and "Throw the oil from the vessel out in the garden." Strangely, only this story moved me.

My grandfather had come to Tokyo when it was still known by the old name of Edo. My father graduated from a medical school in Tokyo. There is a bronze statue of the president of that school at Yujima Tenjin Shrine. The first day I was ever in Tokyo, I was shown that statue; it made me feel strange. A bronze statue gives the queer impression of being almost alive, so I was embarrassed to stare at it.

My grandmother's funeral was the year I entered elementary school. My grandmother, who along with my grandfather had raised me, died just when she could have relaxed her efforts to care for me, a rather sickly child. It rained hard the day of the funeral, so I was carried to the cemetery on the back of some man. My sister, eleven or twelve years old at the time and wearing white clothes, was also being carried on someone's back ahead of me up the red clay mountain path.

My grandmother's death awakened in me my first real feelings for our family altar. When my grandfather was not looking, I stole glances at the bright family altar in its special room. Over and over when my grandfather was unaware, I opened the sliding door a tiny crack, then closed it again. I remember that I hated opening the sliding partition all the way and actually approaching the altar. Whenever I look out at the subdued radiance of the sun as it bathes the mountaintops after dropping just below the horizon, I think of the light in the family altar as it looked to me when I was eight years old. In my graceless first-grader's hand, I had scrawled my grandmother's long, posthumous Buddhist name on the white sliding partition to the altar room; those characters remained there until we sold the house.

Years later, the only thing I can recall of my sister's appearance is the image of her white mourning clothes as she was carried on a man's back. Even if I close my eyes and try to attach a head and limbs to that image, only the rain and the red clay of the path come back to me. I feel irritated that the view in my mind's eye does not parallel the actual events. The man who carried her would not materialize, either. And so this soft white entity floating through the air is the only memory I have of my sister.

My sister was raised at a relative's house from the time I was four or five and died there when I was eleven or twelve. Just as I do not know the essence of my father and mother, I do not know my sister's. My grandfather urged me, "Grieve. Grieve for your sister's death!" I searched my heart, but I was confused, not knowing how to surrender my soul to grief. Seeing my old, feeble grandfather, his sorrow reaching the limit—that was what truly pierced my heart. My emotions gravitated toward my grandfather and lodged there, never attempting to move beyond him to my sister.

My grandfather had studied and excelled in the arts of divination. His eyes troubled him, and in his last years he was nearly blind. When he heard my sister was on the verge of death, he quietly counted his divining rods and divined his granddaughter's life. His eyesight was so weak that he needed me to assist him in lining up the divining blocks. I stared at my grandfather's aged face as the day gradually grew dark. When word of my sister's death came two or three days later, I could not bear to tell my grandfather. I hid the message for two or three hours before finally deciding to read it to him. By that age I could read basic Chinese characters, but when I came across characters written in cursive style that I could not understand, I usually took my grandfather's hand and traced the characters in his palm over and over until he could decipher them. Even now, when I remember the feel of my grandfather's hand as I held it and read him that letter, the palm of my left hand turns cold.

My grandfather died the evening of the funeral of the Empress Dowager. It was the summer of my sixteenth year. When he took a breath, phlegm stopped up his windpipe. He clawed at his chest. One old woman at his bedside said, "He was like a Buddha. Why does he have to suffer so in his last moments?" I could not stand to watch his agony, so I fled to another room for the next hour. A year or so later one of my female cousins reprimanded me for showing such a lack of feeling for my closest living relative. I was silent. I was not surprised that my actions should have been interpreted that way. When I was a boy, I did not like explaining myself. The old woman's words had wounded me so deeply, I thought even a word of explanation as to why I left my grandfather's side as death approached would expose him to disgrace. Then, when

I listened to my cousin's words in silence, the loneliness that had stayed at a distance suddenly sank deep inside me. It was the feeling that I was all alone.

On the day of the funeral, while in the middle of receiving the many funeral guests, I suddenly developed a nosebleed. When I felt the blood start running down my nostrils, I quickly grabbed my nose with the end of my kimono sash and dashed out barefoot across the flagstones in the garden. I lay face up in the shadow of the tree, on a large stone about three feet high in the garden where no one could see me, waiting for my nosebleed to stop. Dazzling sunlight spilled through the leaves of the old oak tree, and I could glimpse small fragments of blue sky. I think that was the first time in my life I had ever had a nosebleed. That nosebleed made me aware of how pained I was over my grandfather's death. As the only member of the family to receive visitors and tend to the funeral matters, I had no time to myself. I had not yet been able to ponder my grandfather's death or how his death would affect my future. I did not consider myself a weakling, but the nosebleed discouraged me. I did not want my sudden disappearance to be interpreted as weakness. I was the chief mourner, and it was almost time for the coffin to be brought out. My behavior was inexcusable and caused a great commotion. There on the garden stone, for the first time in the three days since my grandfather's death, I had a quiet moment to myself. A vague sense that I was forsaken grew in my heart.

The next morning I went to the ceremonial gathering of ashes with six or seven relatives and fellow villagers. There was no roof over the mountain crematory. When we turned over the ashes, a layer of fire still smoldered beneath. As we picked up the bones out of the fire, my nose began to bleed again. I threw down the bamboo fire chopsticks. Mumbling just a word or two, I loosened my sash, held my nose, and dashed up the mountain. I ran to the top. Unlike the day before, my nose would not stop bleeding, no matter what I did. My hands and half the length of my kimono sash were covered with blood, which dripped onto the blades of grass. As I lay quietly on my back, I looked down toward the pond at the foot of the mountain. The morning sun dancing on the surface of the water reflected onto me from far away and made me feel dizzy. My eyes grew weak. About thirty minutes later I heard distant voices calling me repeatedly. I fretted about my sash, which was soaked with blood. But hoping no one would notice since it was black, I returned to the crematory. Everyone's eyes were filled with reproach. The bones had been uncovered, and they told me to pick them up. With a desolate heart, I picked up the small bones. I wore the sash the rest of the day, stiff though it was with dried blood. My second nosebleed was over without its being discovered. I never told anyone about it. Until now, I have neither told any stories about my family nor even once asked anyone about them.

I was raised in the countryside, far from the city, so it would not be much of an exaggeration to say that all fifty families in our village pitied and wept for me. The villagers stood at each crossroads, waiting as the funeral procession advanced. As I passed before them, walking just ahead of the casket, the women wailed loudly. I could hear them crying, "How pathetic, how tragic." I was embarrassed and walked stiffly. After I passed one crossroads, the women standing there took a shortcut in order to stand sobbing again at the next one.

Since my childhood, the sympathies of those around

me have threatened to make me into an object of pity. Half of my heart meekly accepted the blessings from the hearts of others, while the other half haughtily rejected them. After my grandfather's funeral, the funerals of my grandfather's younger sister, of my uncle, of my teacher, and of others close to me caused me to grieve. As for the formal clothes that my father left me, only once did I wear them on a joyful occasion—my cousin's wedding. All the countless other times, I wore them to the cemetery. They made me a master of funerals.

3

The third funeral of that summer vacation was in a village about a mile from my cousin's house. I traveled to my cousin's home as if I were simply going for a visit. I stayed one night. When I was about to leave, a member of my cousin's family smiled as he spoke to me. "We may have to call you again. We have a girl with tuberculosis who may not survive the summer.

"I wonder if we could even hold a funeral without the master?"

I wrapped my formal clothes in a bundle and returned to the home of my cousin in Settsu. My cousin's wife was in the garden. Smiling, she seemed to be in a good humor.

"Welcome home, Mr. Mortician."

"Stop the silly talk. Bring some salt," I said, standing up straight at the gate.

"Salt? What are you going to do with it?"

"I'm going to purify myself. I can't go inside unless I do."

"How disgusting. It's like a neurosis."

She brought a handful of salt and sprinkled it on me with a theatrical flourish.

"Is that enough?"

My cousin was about to put the slightly sweaty kimono I had just taken off out on the sunlit veranda to dry. She sniffed at it, furrowing her eyebrows at me. Recalling a joke, she said, "How horrible. Your kimono smells like a grave."

"What a wicked thing to say! You don't even have a clue what a grave smells like."

My cousin was still smiling. "Yes, I do. It smells like burnt hair."

GATHERING ASHES

There were two ponds in the valley.

The lower pond glimmered, as if brimming with molten silver, while the upper pond was deep and silent like death, as though the mountain shadows lay submerged in the green waters.

My face was sticky. Looking back at the path I had made, I found that blood had fallen on the bamboo grass and weeds. The drops of blood looked as if they might move.

My nose began to bleed again, the blood pulsing in warm waves.

I quickly pressed my kimono sash to my nose and lay down on my back, looking up at the sky.

The undersides of the leaves dazzled me as the sun struck them from above.

The blood stopped halfway down inside my nose and began to run back; it was an unpleasant sensation. It tickled and made the inside of my nose itch when I breathed.

The cicadas suddenly burst out screeching all over the hill, as if startled.

This late morning in July—it seemed as though even

the drop of a pin might cause it all to disintegrate. I felt I could not move my body.

As I lay there sweating, the screeching of the cicadas, the green pressing in around me, the warmth of the earth, and the beating of my heart all converged at a single point inside my head. Then, even as I sensed them converge, they dissipated.

I felt as though I would be drawn up into the sky.

"Get down here."

I leapt to my feet at the sound of a voice shouting from the crematory.

It was the morning after my grandfather's funeral ceremony. We had come for the gathering of the ashes. While the others were stirring through the ashes, still warm from the cremation, my nose had begun to bleed. I had held my nose with the end of my sash and fled the crematory, climbing the hill to escape notice.

I ran back down the hill when I was called. The pond that glimmered like silver flickered, then disappeared. I slipped on last year's dead leaves.

"You certainly took your time. Where were you? Your grandfather is a Buddha now. Take a look." My old aunt spoke as she stepped out of the crematory.

"Really? Where?" I shuffled through the bamboo grass. I worried about my color and about my blood-soaked sash after my heavy nosebleed. Nevertheless, I approached my aunt.

A small cinder attracted everyone's attention. It was about an inch in diameter and lay resting on a white sheet in the old woman's hand. Her hand looked like a crumpled piece of brown paper.

I understood that the cinder was his Adam's apple. With some effort, I could even imagine it as a human shape.

"We just found it. Well, this is what your grandfather looks like now. Come put this in the urn."

How trivial! My grandfather should be waiting to hear me open the gate to our house, his blind eyes filled with joy at the sound. How odd to have this woman standing here—a woman I have never seen before who claims she is my aunt.

The bones of his feet, his hands, and his neck were all tossed randomly into the urn.

This crematory was small, with no wall around it and only a long, narrow hole in which to cremate a body.

The heat from the ashes was intense.

"Well, let's go to the grave. It stinks in here. Besides, the sunlight coming in is dirty yellow." I spoke, fretting about my spinning head and my nose, which threatened to bleed again.

When I looked back, the old man from the crematory was carrying the urn under his arm. The remaining ashes and the straw mats that only yesterday had been covered with funeral guests at the incense burning were all left untouched. The bamboo stood with silver paper still attached.

At the wake the night before, my grandfather became a spirit of blue flame. He flew out through the roof of the shrine, floated through the rooms of the nearby quarantine hospital, and left a disagreeable odor as he drifted through the village sky. Walking to the grave, I recalled this story.

The crematory was in one corner of the village cemetery, but my family's gravesite was in a separate area.

We arrived at my family's gravesite, where the stone monuments stood.

I did not care. I wanted to tumble to the ground and breathe in the blue sky.

My old aunt set down a big copper kettle of water she had brought from the valley. "According to his last will and testament, he wanted to be buried beneath the stone of his oldest ancestors." She pronounced the words "last will and testament" with utmost gravity.

The old woman's two sons pushed their way through the people, overturned the ancient stone monument at the highest spot, and dug a hole beneath it.

The hole seemed rather deep. The urn echoed at the bottom as though it had fallen a great distance.

After death they put your cinders in your ancestors' grave. When you die, there is nothing—only a life that will be forgotten.

The stone monument was put back in its place.

"Well, boy, this is good-bye."

The old woman tossed water on the small stone monument. The incense smoked, but it cast no shadow in the relentless sunlight. The flowers were wilted.

Everyone prayed, palms pressed together, eyes closed.

I looked at their yellow faces. I felt faint again.

My grandfather's life—and death.

I shook my right hand back and forth as if a spring were attached.

The bones rattled. I was carrying the smaller urn.

"He was an unfortunate man." "A man who did everything for his family." "A man who will not be forgotten by his village." Such was the talk of grandfather on the way back. I wish they would stop. I am the only one who is grieving.

And the people who had stayed behind at the house were wondering what would become of me now that I was left alone. However, I sensed curiosity mingled with their sympathy.

A peach fell to the ground. It rolled to my feet. We

had skirted the foot of Peach Mountain on the way home from the grave.

This is an event from my sixteenth year that I wrote down in my eighteenth (1916). Now I have recopied it, revising the wording a bit.

It intrigues me now at the age of fifty-one to reread something that I wrote when I was eighteen. Just to think that I am still alive.

My grandfather died on May 24, but "Gathering Ashes" is set in July. I see now there was some fiction involved.

This story appeared in *Bunsho Nikki*, published by Shinchosha, but one sheet had been torn out and lost. Between the lines "the heat of the ashes was intense" and "well, let's go to the grave," two pages were missing from my diary. Nevertheless, I copied it without those missing pages.

Before I came across "Gathering Ashes," I found a piece entitled "To My Home Village," in which I addressed as "you" the village where I had lived with my grandfather. It took the form of a letter written from my middle-school dormitory. It was merely youthful sentimentality.

I shall pick up the connection between "Gathering Ashes" and "To My Home Village":

" . . . although I had vowed otherwise to you, the other day at my uncle's house I consented to selling the house in which my grandfather and I had lived.

"A few days ago you probably saw the trunk and wardrobe from the storage room being handed over to a buyer.

"After I left you, I heard that my home became a shelter for poor vagrants, and since the wife of the crazy man next door died of rheumatism, it is being used as a jail for him.

"Other things in the storage room will eventually be stolen. The cemetery hill will gradually be cut away and become part of Peach Mountain. The third anniversary of Grandfather's death is approaching, but his memorial tablet in the Buddhist altar has probably tumbled into the rat urine."

TWO

HURRAH

The elder sister was twenty and the younger seventeen. They both worked at the same hot spring but for different inns. Both of them were extremely beautiful and delicate. They seldom went out. But they did see each other occasionally at the village theater.

There was a performance about once every two months—during the Bon Festival in the summer, at New Year's, during the farmers' off-season, on holidays, and during the village festivals. Itinerant entertainers came to the village and performed, usually for three days at a time. When the maids at the inns had enough free time, they would go see the shows two nights in a row. Naturally, the two sisters would run into each other, even if they had not arranged to meet. They would talk for a moment, then would separate, each to take her own seat. The two sisters looked so much alike and were so beautiful that they were distressed by everyone's stares. Even when they were apart, people talked about them.

"One of the actors said he wanted them to be sure to sit together. He said it is hard to make eyes at both of them if they sit apart."

But when a movie was playing, the two beauties

watched it together. When the show was over and the lights came on, they both blushed and lowered their faces.

A man staying at the older sister's inn and a woman staying at the younger sister's inn became acquainted. The man made the first move.

"Where are you from?"

"I don't have a hometown."

"Have you been staying here long?"

"Yes, a month."

"Will you be staying here for a while?"

"I'm not sure. I know almost all of the hot springs in Japan west of here, and this is the most boring place I have seen yet. I've been stuck here for a month."

The woman chattered about her impressions of twenty different inns, one after another.

"I'm the daughter of a traveling entertainer. That's how I have risen so high in the world," she laughed.

The fifth or sixth time they met, she finally asked him a favor.

"Would you take me to another inn? If you would only take me to the next inn, that would be enough. And then if you grow tired of me, you may leave."

The woman told him her life's dream. Her father was an entertainer who had traveled the inns at the hot springs around the southern provinces. She longed to see all the hot springs throughout Japan. So she had made up her mind to undertake this wretched journey. At one inn she would wait for a man who would take her to the next. There she would search for another man to take her to a hot spring farther north. In this fashion she had traveled north, the number of springs equal to the number of escorts she had met.

"I've been here for an entire month. I feel sorry for you, having to put up with my irritability and melancholy every day. But I don't want to die like a beggar before I reach the hot spring at the northernmost point in Hokkaido. I wonder how many hot springs there will be between here and there. I must make it there while I'm still young; no one will take me once I'm old."

The man spoke cheerfully. "Wonderful. I will buy your daydream."

An open car was waiting.

Several maids from the two inns had come out to see the man and the woman off. The two sisters met beside the car.

As the car carrying the man and the woman started off, she turned around in the seat, waved a bouquet of miscanthus expansively, and exclaimed, "Hurrah, hurrah, hurrah!"

"Good-bye."

"Good-bye," one maid called out. Then encouraged by the woman's shout, she cried, "Hurrah!"

"Hurrah!" Six or seven others cried, also infected.

"Hurrah!"

"Hurrah!"

"Hurrah!"

The woman kept shouting as she sped away in the distance, "Hurrah, hurrah, hurrah!"

The two sisters joined hands as they shrieked and shook with laughter. Thet glanced at each other; they wanted to hug each other and dance. But instead, they joined hands and, lifting their arms high in the air, shouted joyously.

"Hurrah!"

"Hurrah!"

THE PRINCESS OF THE DRAGON PALACE

"Make my gravestone taller than the woman. Force her to embrace the stone and bury them both in the sea."

In his last desperate moments, the father spoke these words, so his two sons ordered a splendid monument made. The father was murdered in a terribly cruel manner at the hands of his young wife and her lover.

The sons, children by his first wife, nimbly carried the gravestone to a precipice above the ocean. The stone was taller than the woman, their enemy. The cliff was so terrifying that when they dropped a rock, it grew smaller as it fell, until it looked no larger than a sesame seed; but they became dizzy and had to stop watching before it hit the water. Then the sons stripped the woman, bound her to the monument with a coarse rope, and gave the stone a heave. Instinctively, the woman wrapped her arms and legs around the monument. It groaned like a living creature and tumbled over the edge.

Then, let's see, what happened next? Halfway down the cliff, in the blink of an eye, the stone seemed to stop.

And wouldn't you know, with the woman straddling its back, the gravestone skimmed along like a sled over snow. When it was about to plunge into the ocean, it was transformed into a beautiful small boat that rushed toward the offing like a streak of light. Seeing this, the two sons clung to each other. "Father, forgive us," they cried and collapsed to the ground.

The woman's lover ran to the cliff's edge. Her boat was swift as a swallow darting through the air. No ordinary boat could catch her. He ran to the husband's grave and carried the monument foundation stone back to the cliff. Holding it, he hurled himself toward the sea. And, indeed, the stone turned into a boat that sped away like a streak of light.

The man's boat caught up with the woman's. He spoke to her.

"We must now thank the man we killed."

"We can't. We must not thank my husband. If you have any feeling of gratitude in your heart, your boat will turn back into a gravestone."

Before the woman had finished speaking, the man's boat turned into a gravestone and sank toward the bottom of the sea.

Seeing this, the woman spoke. "Oh, boat of mine! Turn to stone and follow my beloved beneath the sea!"

Embracing the monument, the naked woman dove beneath the surface like a mermaid.

But, offended that he should sink alone to the bottom, the man called out, "Gravestone! Change into a boat and float back up to the surface of the sea to the boat of my beloved."

Halfway down, he began to rise, having made his request of the man he had helped kill with his own hands.

Then, let's see, what happened next? The woman sinking and the man rising passed each other in the sea. Finally, the woman sank to the bottom alone.

And that woman became the princess of the palace of the dragon king.

When she told me this fairy tale, I thought she was going to commit a lover's suicide herself. And, indeed, she did jump into the sea with her lover. The man died. But she was revived, and in that instant, she cried out and clung to the husband she had deceived. Later, when I saw her again, she said, "It was just like the fairy tale. To the very end—exactly the same!"

THE MONEY ROAD

This occurred on September 1, 1924.

"Hey, Granny. It's about time we went out."

Kenta—Ken, as he was called—the shrewd beggar, pulled a pair of worn-out army boots from the wood shavings.

"Do you know about that foreign god? The one who puts good fortune in your shoes while you're sleeping? At the end of the year they have all those socks hanging around for sale? That's the one I mean."

Ken turned the boots upside down and knocked the dust out of them as he spoke.

"I wonder how much money I would have if these were full of silver coins. A hundred yen, maybe a thousand."

The old woman, leaning against a plastered wall that had not yet dried, absentmindedly fingered a red comb.

"It was probably a young girl," she said.

"Who?"

"The person who lost the comb."

"Who else would it be?"

"She was probably sixteen or seventeen. I suppose you saw her."

"Stop it, Granny. You're thinking about your dead daughter again."

"It's been a year today since she died."

"So you're going to make a memorial visit to the ruins of the Military Clothing Depot, right?"

"When I go to the Military Clothing Depot, I'm going to make an offering of this comb for my daughter."

"That's fine. . . . And Granny, it's all right to remember your daughter, but, well, can't you think about when you were young yourself? Last night when I came back and went upstairs, a man and woman jumped up out of the wood shavings. It was warm there where they had been. I lay down in the warmth and waited for you. Then you go and pick up some red comb and just cry and cry. We've been beggars together now for almost a whole year. Just once before I die, I want to make you young again and for us to be a couple. These days, you know, young people sneak into these construction sites to make love. And I'm not even fifty yet myself."

"I'm fifty-six. My late husband was two years younger than I. You know, I had a dream. All the people who died at the clothing depot, thousands, tens of thousands, they all were crossing a long bridge. They say paradise is far away."

"Well, let's go together. We can drink sweet sake tonight. We'll go there and I'll loan you my left boot. It'll be easier to use your right foot."

Ken slipped on his army boots, stood up, and brushed the wood shavings off the old woman's back.

The old woman's family had all burned to death in the clothing depot after the great earthquake in Tokyo on September 1, the year before.

She was offered relief in the barracks run by the city in Asakusa Park.

Ken, the shrewd beggar, who had made his home in Asakusa, pretended to be a victim in the confusion following the earthquake to receive free clothing and food. When the freeloaders were chased out of the barracks, Ken talked the lonely old woman into registering him as her husband's younger brother. But the city office was not about to keep feeding men who were able to work. Fortunately the beggar's spirit made him resilient. He left the Okami Relief Center in two or three months.

The old woman could not part from Ken. She had come to depend on him, so the two begged together. They tramped around half of Tokyo, staying in houses under construction to keep off the rain and dew.

On the anniversary of the earthquake an imperial messenger appeared at the ruins of the clothing depot. The prime minister, the interior minister, and the mayor all read memorial addresses at the ceremony. Foreign ambassadors sent memorial wreaths.

At 11:58 all traffic stopped, and the people of the city observed a moment of silence.

Steamships that had gathered from Yokohama made the trip up and down the Sumida River to the bank near the clothing depot. The automobile companies vied to be first to make an official appearance in front of the clothing depot. Each religious organization, Red Cross hospital, and Christian girls school sent a relief committee to the ceremony.

A postcard dealer rounded up some vagrants and dispatched a squad to secretly sell photographs of bodies mangled in the earthquake. A movie studio technician walked around with a tall tripod. Money changers stood in a row to change the visitors' silver coins for lesser copper coins to be tossed into the offering box.

Uniformed youth corps members policed the streets. Funeral draperies hung from the eaves of the barrack houses to the east of Azuma Bridge and Ryokoku Bridge. Visitors there were served spring water, milk, biscuits, boiled eggs, and shaved ice.

The scene of the epilogue to last year's tragedy: jostled among the crowd of hundreds of thousands, Ken lugged the old woman's arm under his own as if it were a package. In front of a tall gate whose unfinished wood pillars were wrapped with black-and-white-striped funeral draperies, Ken quickly told the old woman to put on his left boot.

"Take off your right sandal. It's best if you go barefoot."

They were forced along the fenced-off road, pressed against each other, step by step moving closer to the charnel house. Beyond the people's heads a dark shower was falling.

"Look at that, Granny. That's all money. It's raining money."

Just as a brilliant forest of floral wreaths and funeral greenery came into view, their feet suddenly felt cold. It was coins.

"Ow."

"Ouch."

People crouched to protect their heads. Coins. At their feet were copper coins, copper coins, silver coins. The ground was covered with coins. They were walking on coins. A mountain of coins had accumulated before the white cotton draperies in front of the charnel house. Unable to move forward, the throngs had not waited until they reached the charnel house to make their offerings. They had thrown the money from where they stood. Now coins were falling like hail on everyone's heads.

"Granny, do you understand how smart I am? I am asking you to do your best."

Ken's voice trembled. He busily picked up coins with the toes of his left foot and dropped them into his big right boot.

The closer they advanced to the charnel house on the cold money road, the deeper the layer of coins grew. People were walking an inch off the ground.

They escaped to safety on a deserted bank of the big river, dragging the heavy boots. When they squatted beneath a rusty tin roof, they were surprised to see the number of boats and people. It looked as though it were opening day on the river.

"Oh, now I can die. I've walked on a money road. It's just too much. Too much. My foot is cramped like I've walked on a mountain of needles in hell."

In contrast to Ken's pale face, the old woman appeared blushing and youthful.

"My heart was aflutter like a young girl's, Ken—the wonderful feeling of walking on silver coins. It was like some nice man was biting the sole of my foot."

The old woman took off the left boot. Ken shouted in amazement when he looked inside.

"What? You didn't pick up anything but silver coins!"

"Do you think I'm so stupid I would pick up copper coins?"

"That's incredible."

Ken stared into the old woman's face.

"Sure enough, it was my beggar's spirit. Even in a crowd so dense I couldn't see my own belt, you could still sort out the silver from the copper. I couldn't walk on the coins. My feet cramped up after I'd picked up just ten."

"What are you talking about? Go ahead and count it up."

"Fifty sen, sixty sen, eighty sen, ninety sen, one yen forty sen—twenty-one yen thirty sen. And there's even more."

"Ken, I forgot to offer the comb for my daughter. It's still here tucked in my sleeve."

"Your daughter won't rest until you do."

"I'll throw it in the river. I'll put it in this boot and throw it in the river as an offering for her."

The old woman flung her arm out wide like a young girl and tossed the boot in the river.

"We can count the money tomorrow, Ken. Let's buy sake. Let's buy sea bream. Tonight is my—my wedding. Is that all right, Ken? Why are you sitting there in a daze? Oh, you . . ."

The old woman's eyes became moist with a mysteriously youthful color.

The red comb floated out of the sinking boot and silently drifted down the great river.

CHASTITY UNDER THE ROOF

"I'll be waiting for you on the hill in the park at four o'clock."

"I'll be waiting for you on the hill in the park at four o'clock."

"I'll be waiting for you on the hill in the park at four o'clock."

She sent the same letter by special delivery to three men—one who walked with a cane, one who wore glasses, and one with neither glasses nor a cane.

At three o'clock in the afternoon on the hill, she quietly blossomed like a moonflower. All around her were new buds that had let the morning air touch their infant skin for the first time and now grieved on the tips of the tree branches that the first night of their lives should come.

The man with a cane climbed the hill. Surely the handle of his cane had detected the truth—that she sent special-delivery letters to several men each day and that the first man to come would be hers for the night.

She flashed a beautiful smile, like one who had just been born into this world. As she ran down the hill on innocent heels, she closed her eyes solemnly and crossed herself in front of her face.

"God, I am grateful that through this person you have blessed a child like me with another peaceful night's rest. And if I live until tomorrow, I pray that, through one of your children, I may again be granted another night's lodging."

As she nestled close to the man, the houses in the city looked up at her with cold indifference from the bottom of the hill. She gazed out over them and spoke as if dazzled.

"You roofs. Roofs. Roofs. You countless roofs who push your tiny heads against the sky. You guardian deities of a woman's chastity, each of you mercifully defending each woman's honor. I spend each night beneath a different roof. And for each roof, how chastely I sleep that night. Oh, which roof will be mine tonight? But this night's roof will be the only one not angry with me, and so . . . "

The woman and the man disappeared into the town.

THE MOON

Virginity—what an insufferable nuisance you are! You are baggage I would never miss. And as I walk along dusky back streets or bridges, it would be nothing to me to simply dump you into a trash can or river. But now that I have emerged onto the brightly lit paved street, I am afraid it will be hard to find a place to dispose of you. Moreover, when women marvel at my baggage, curious about what is inside, don't I blush? And just because I have carried it all this way, my thoughts so heavy, don't I feel that I can't just give it to some dog on the roadside? But these days, now that so many women have tried to love me, my incessant discomfort has only increased, as though I am wearing high clogs that dig into the snow as I walk. How much lighter my feelings would be if I could run barefoot across the snow.

These were his thoughts.

One woman stood by his pillow, but then dropped roughly to her knees. She leaned over him and breathed in his scent.

Another woman clung to him when he pretended to give her a push. She was leaning against the railing of a second-floor balcony. But when he let go, she looked again as if she were going to fall, leaning backward over the rail. Staring at her own chest, she waited for him.

Another woman's hand began to tremble as she held onto his shoulder. She was rinsing his back in the bath.

Another woman unexpectedly dashed out into the garden when the two of them were sitting in a parlor in the winter. She lay face up on the sofa in the arbor house, her elbows wrapped firmly over her face.

And one woman stopped dead still when he grabbed her jokingly from behind.

One woman clamped her lips shut, stiffened her body, and turned away when he took hold of her hand as she pretended to be asleep.

Another woman brought her sewing into his room late one night while he was out and settled herself in like a stone. When he returned, she blushed and told him she was just borrowing his light. Hers was an uncanny, husky voice, as though a lie were caught in her throat.

Another woman always cried when she faced him.

While they were talking to him, very young women gradually lapsed into personal, emotional stories. Then, when they could say no more, they sat down as though they had lost the strength to stand.

When that time came, he would descend into a white silence. If not, he would always say the same thing:

"I have decided I will not be moved by any woman except one who intends to join her life with mine."

After he turned twenty-five, women like these became more and more common. And consequently, the wall surrounding his virginity grew more and more solid.

But one woman went so far as to tell him that it had become disagreeable to look upon faces other than his. She passed her days bewildered. He thought this woman might starve to death if he did not nurture her. And he sensed that the women whom he would have to nurture, who would not join their lives with his, by whom he would not be moved, would increase in number. He smiled.

"If I do that, having so few assets, I'll soon be bankrupt."

Then perhaps, as he had so many times before, he would venture forth like a beggar, carrying only his baggage of virginity. Looking poverty-stricken, nonetheless emotionally rich because he had only taken while giving away nothing, astride a donkey, bound for a distant country . . .

Toying with such daydreams, his chest swelled with the emotions inside him. But he could no longer imagine he would be able to find a woman in this world who would join her life with his.

Looking up, he saw a full moon. It was so bright that it looked like the only being in the sky. He stretched both hands toward the moon.

"Oh, moon! I offer these emotions to you!"

ENEMY

The screen actress shed great tears in the dim light while watching a movie in which she played the lead role.

In her life, the actress's parents had been her first enemies. Her older brother was her next. And so, from that time on, she saw every person in the world as an enemy. Men were particularly her enemies. Every time her enemies increased by one, she took another step down into a dark abyss.

Now, on the movie screen, the most pitiful young girl in the world was being sold to a man by her parents.

The girl watching and the girl being watched—the two of them cried simultaneously. And as the film rolled by, together they felt the sorrow of losing their virginity.

She was not just recalling that dreadful time in her past; she felt as though she were experiencing it again now. And even when they filmed this scene, she had not been acting; she had felt as though she were reliving that horrible event with her entire body.

In other words, up to now she had lost her virginity three times. In other words, she had been three times a virgin.

In the throes of her third sorrow, a man and a woman

were ushered to the seats in front of hers. Without thinking, she started to speak to them. It was an actress and a director from her studio.

Immediately, the actress in front of her turned to the director as if to superimpose her white profile onto the tearful face on the screen. She whispered to him.

"Look at that. She doesn't look like a naive virgin. Her body has lost all its form. Oh, and there, her breasts . . ."

"Ah! I can't kill her!" She slid off the seat and onto the floor on one knee, as if driving a blade into the floor.

For the first time in her life, the actress had encountered a true enemy.

The fourth time she lost her virginity was by this other actress—and this time without leaving a trace, not a shadow.

A man can never rob a woman of her virginity.

A WOMAN

A Zen priest in a castle town had a head shaped like a gourd. He addressed a samurai who came in through the temple gate.

"I wonder if you saw a fire on your way here."

"A woman had collapsed in tears. She said she was crying because her husband had been burned to death. It was a pathetic sight."

"Ha, ha, ha. Her crying was fake."

"What do you mean?"

"They were crocodile tears. She was rejoicing that her husband had died. Most likely she has another man. They probably got him drunk, killed him by driving needles into his head, then set fire to the house."

"Is there some rumor to that effect?"

"No. No rumor. It's that crying of hers."

"Her crying?"

"Some people have the ears of a Buddha."

"I see. If that is true, then she is an abominable woman!"

The young samurai rolled his eyes and dashed back out the temple gate.

A short while later he returned, his face pale.

"Priest."

"What is it?"

"I brought her to justice. I struck her down with a single slash of my sword."

"Ha, ha, ha, ha, ha. You did?"

"But, the moment I saw my sword flash, I began to doubt your words. The woman was clinging to the charred corpse, wailing as loudly as she could. She clasped her hands together and thanked me. 'Would you kill me?' she said. 'Would you send me where my husband has gone?' She thanked me and died smiling."

"I suppose so. It must be true."

"What are you saying?"

"When I passed, her crying was fake. When you passed, it was genuine."

"For a priest, you deceive people a great deal."

"It's just that you do not have the ears of a Buddha."

"I have sullied the sword of a warrior. What should I do about this stain?"

"Purify it and present it to me. Draw your sword."

"To cut off your gourd-shaped head?"

"That would sully it again."

"Nevertheless . . ."

"First hand it to me."

The priest took the naked blade. With a shout, he hurled it at a stone monument in the cemetery. It pierced a tombstone. Red blood oozed from the stone.

"Oh, oh!"

"It is the blood of the man who was killed."

"The man's blood?"

"It is the blood of the woman who was killed."

"What? Are you trying to torment me with sorcery?"

"It is not sorcery. That gravestone belongs to the ancestors of the house that burned."

The samurai began to tremble.

"Priest. That is a celebrated sword that has been passed down through generations in my family . . . "

"Well, then, why don't you pull it out."

The samurai placed both hands on the sword and yanked. The stone tumbled over, and in that instant the blade broke in two. Not even a mark as small as a fingernail scratch was left on the stone. Smooth green moss covered its surface.

"What's this? It's uncanny."

The samurai slumped back on the ground and gazed vacantly at the broken sword. The priest turned and walked toward the main sanctuary.

"It's about time for services to begin."

FRIGHTENING LOVE

He had loved his wife intensely. In other words, he had loved this one woman too much. He considered his wife's early death to be a punishment from heaven for his love. This was the only sense he could make of her death.

After she died, he stayed far away from any kind of woman. He would not even hire a woman to care for his house. He employed men do the cooking and cleaning. It was not that he hated all other women, but simply that any woman reminded him of his wife. For example, to him every woman smelled of fish, just as his wife had. Wondering if this feeling itself was also heaven's punishment for loving his wife too much, he resigned himself to a life without a trace of a woman.

But there lived in his house one woman he could do nothing about. He had a daughter. And, of course, she looked more like his late wife than any woman in the world.

The girl began to attend middle school.

Once, when the light came on in the girl's room in the middle of the night, he peeped through a crack in the sliding partition. The girl was holding a small pair of scissors. Her knees were drawn up and spread apart as she used the scissors, looking down for a long time. The next day, after the girl had gone to school, he shuddered as he secretly stared at the white scissor blades.

Another night, the light in the girl's room came on again. He peeked through the crack in the partition. The girl folded a white cloth and carried it out of the room. He could hear the sound of water running. Soon the girl started a fire in the charcoal brazier. Placing the white cloth on top, she sat beside it. Then she burst into tears. When she stopped, she began to trim her nails over the cloth. The nails fell as she removed the cloth. The smell of burning nails nauseated him.

He had a dream. He dreamed that his dead wife told his daughter that he had seen her secret.

The daughter stopped looking at his face. He did not love his daughter. He shuddered when he thought that some man would be punished by heaven one day for loving this girl.

Finally, one night, a dagger in her hand, the girl eyed her father's throat. He knew it. His eyes closed in resignation. This was his punishment for loving his wife intensely, for loving one woman too much. Knowing that the girl would attack her mother's enemy, he waited for the blade.

HORSE BEAUTY

"There is no one in the world as generous as I. I gave my husband to someone else. Ha, ha, ha, ha, ha!"

Shaking her barrel of a belly, the girl's mother laughed like the blue sky. Even if she had wanted to grieve, her belly would not allow it. Her heart was light, lifted by bright balloons that filled her belly.

"There is no one in the world as generous as I. I gave my daughter, my horse, and my home all to my wife."

Perhaps this is what the girl's father had said. He was living with his mistress in a small place on the outskirts of the village.

The mother's house stood in a field. Behind it, a bamboo grove made little dancing waves of sunlight. Corn hung like lanterns from the eaves of the old house, and cosmos bloomed in the garden. A white rooster flapped his wings in the patch of cosmos as if trying to sever the weak stems of the flowers.

A horse hung his head out from the stable over these artificial-looking flowers. The father had left the horse behind when he moved away because it was needed here. The young men of the village called the man's daughter the "horse beauty."

The horse beauty knew a man when she was sixteen.

There were only two eyes in this village that moved like points of light, and both belonged to the horse beauty. Her eyes were dark, her voice deep as a man's, husky, like the voice of a sumo wrestler who has broken his Adam's apple. Moreover, it became more masculine with the years. But, for the horse beauty, this masculinity seemed only to enhance her femininity. That was obvious from the agitation she caused among the young men.

One morning in May the horse beauty was out in the rice paddies with her mother. Her mother was trudging along, gripping the handles of the horse-drawn plow. The blade kept coming out of the ground. Seeing this, the girl lunged into the field like a wild bronco, splashing muddy water all over her back.

"You idiot!" She slapped her mother's face. "What do you think you're doing? You don't just dabble in the water. You turn over the soil! The soil!"

Her mother stopped and held her cheek. Dragged forward by the plow she still gripped with her right hand, she staggered and laughed, her belly shaking, but more sadly this time than when her husband left her. She spoke to the villagers in the next paddy.

"My daughter has a lot of husbands, but I am her only wife. It's just too much for me."

The mother said she would go to her husband's house. Deep in debt, he had just sold his wife's house and horse to someone else. He broke with his mistress.

The moonlight was almost audible as it submerged the house and the fields in green light. The mother's great shaking belly subsided. She dreamed about her husband's house, where she would be going the next day. In one dream, the horse beauty leapt up from her bedding and spat on her mother's belly.

That same night the girl mounted the horse bareback in the stable. It trampled the cosmos flowers under its hooves, kicking them about in the moonlight, then galloped off at top speed like a black meteor toward the mountains to the south.

According to one villager—

"I hear she sold the horse in the harbor town and went off to some man's place by boat."

According to her mother—

"My daughter was my husband, but even my daughter ran off after some man."

According to her father—

"It was wrong to give her that nickname 'horse beauty.' That's why she ran away on that horse I had already sold."

And according to one of the young men—

"I saw it. The horse beauty flew off from the top of the mountain like an arrow toward the moon, horse and all."

THE SEA

A band of Koreans in Japan was traveling to a new home over a white mountain road in July. All of them were tired by the time the sea came into view. They had built a road over the mountains. Three years of labor by these seventy people had opened a new road as far as the pass. There was a different contractor for the road construction on the other side, so the Koreans no longer had work.

The women had left the mountain village near dawn. One girl of sixteen or seventeen was overcome by exhaustion, her face white as paper, when she caught sight of the sea.

"My stomach hurts. I can't walk."

"What shall we do? You rest here awhile and come along later with the men."

"Will they be coming?"

"Of course they will. They'll come flowing like a river."

Laughing, the other women headed down toward the sea, carrying bundles and wicker baskets on their backs.

The girl put down her bundle and squatted on the grass.

Ten construction workers passed before her.

"Hey, what's the matter?" they called out to the girl.

"Will someone be coming along after you?"

"Yes."

"My stomach hurts. I'll be along later."

Looking down at the summer sea, the girl felt light-headed. The shrill sound of the cicadas permeated her body. Every time some of the laborers passed by on their way from the mountain village—in fours or sevens or twos—the same thing happened.

"What's the matter?"

"Will someone be coming along after you?"

"Yes."

A young laborer came out of the cedar grove, carrying a large wicker trunk on his back.

"Why are you crying?"

"Will someone else be coming?"

"Someone else? No. I stayed behind until last on purpose. I didn't want to leave the woman."

"Really? No one else is coming?"

"No."

"Really?"

"Don't cry. What's the matter?"

The laborer sat down beside the girl.

"I can't walk. My stomach hurts."

"Oh. I'll carry you. You can be my wife."

"No. My father told me I must not marry in the land where he was killed. I am not to become the bride of someone who has come to this land. He told me to go back to Korea to marry."

"Hmm. So that's why your father died the way he did. Look at your clothes."

"This?" The girl looked down at her summer kimono. It was an autumn grass pattern. "This was a gift. I want train fare and a Korean dress."

"What's in your bundle?"

"Pans and bowls."

"Be my wife."

"Won't someone else be coming along?"

"I'm the last. You could wait three years—there won't be another Korean coming by."

"Really? No one else is coming?"

"Be my wife. . . . You can't walk. I'm going to leave."

"There won't be even one more person coming?"

"That's right, so listen to what I'm saying."

"All right."

"Good."

Holding the girl's shoulders, the laborer stood. They slung their huge parcels onto their backs.

"Are you sure there won't be even one more person coming?"

"Be quiet."

"Please take me where I can't look at the sea."

HANDS

1

The sound of waves grew louder. The man lifted the window curtains. The fires on the fishing boats were visible on the water, but they appeared more distant than they had before. Fog had settled on the ocean.

Looking back at the bed, a chill ran through his chest. The stark white sheets lay flat on the bed. Had his new bride's body sunk deep into the soft mattress? There was not the slightest bulge on the bed. Only her head lay raised on the pillow.

As he gazed at her sleeping, he shed silent tears, though he did not know why.

The bedclothes looked like a sheet of white paper that had fallen in the moonlight. Suddenly, he felt something ominous about the open window. He closed the curtains and walked toward the bed.

Resting his elbow on the bedpost ornament, he peered into his wife's face. He slid his palms down the leg of the bedstead and knelt, pressing his forehead against the round iron post. The metallic chill penetrated his head.

Silently he placed his palms together in the manner of Buddhist devotion.

"Stop it! How horrid! You act as if I were dead."

He sprang to his feet, blushing.

"Have you been awake?"

"I haven't slept a wink. I just keep dreaming."

She thrust her chest out like a bow. The moment she looked at him, the white bedclothes billowed with warmth. He patted the sheets.

"The fog is settling in on the ocean."

"The fishing boats have left by now, haven't they?"

"No, they are still out on the water."

"Didn't you say there was fog?"

"It's all right. It's just a light mist. . . . Well, good night."

He placed a hand on the covers and brought his lips toward hers.

"Stop it. When I'm awake you do this, and when I'm asleep you treat me like a dead person."

2

Pressing his hands together in devotion was a habit from his youth.

Having lost his parents at an early age, he lived with his blind grandfather in a mountain village. His grandfather often brought his young grandson before the family altar. He would grope for the boy's hands and press them together between his own to worship. How cold his grandfather's hands had been.

The boy grew up quite willful and headstrong. He was often unreasonable and made his grandfather cry. Whenever that happened, his grandfather called a priest from the mountain temple. The boy always calmed down when the priest arrived. His grandfather did not know why.

Eyes closed, the priest sat erect, his palms pressed together before the boy. The boy felt a chill when he saw these devotions. After the priest left, the boy would face his grandfather and silently press his palms together. His grandfather could not see him, his blind white eyes open in vain. Yet the boy felt his heart washed clean.

Thus, he came to believe in the power of hands pressed palm to palm. This orphan boy committed many sins as he grew up and took advantage of many people. Still, there were two things his character would not permit him to do: express gratitude or ask forgiveness directly. When he stayed at someone's home, he could not wait for bedtime so he could press his palms together as he did every night in his devotions. He believed that in this way his unexpressed feelings could somehow be communicated to others.

3

In the shadow of the new leaves of the paulownia tree, pomegranate flowers bloomed like burning lights.

A dove returned from the pine grove to the eaves outside the study.

Now at last, near the end of the rainy season, moonbeams began to tremble in the evening breeze.

From noon until midnight he sat fixedly before the

window, his palms pressed together. His wife had left a brief note and run off to her old lover. He prayed she would return.

Gradually his ears could distinguish different sounds around him. He could hear the assistant's whistle at the train station half a mile away. He heard the patter of innumerable feet, like the sound of distant rain. Then, in his mind's eye, he could see his wife.

He went out to the road he had been watching for half a day. His wife was walking there.

"Hey." He tapped her on the shoulder.

She stared at him blankly.

"You've come back. I thought if only you would come back to me, it would be all right."

She fell toward him, leaning on him and rubbing her eyes against his shoulder. He spoke quietly as they walked.

"A while ago you were sitting on a bench at the station, biting on the handle of your parasol."

"Did you see me?"

"I could see you."

"And you didn't say anything?"

"No. I could see you from the window."

"Really?"

"I saw you so I came out to meet you."

"That's spooky."

"Is that all you think? . . . just that it's spooky?"

"No."

"It was about eight-thirty when you started thinking you would come back, wasn't it?"

"That's enough! I'm already dead. I remember. The night I came here as your wife, you bowed and pressed your hands together as you would before a dead person. Then . . . that's when I died."

"Then?"

"I won't leave again. Forgive me."

But now he felt a desire to test his power—to join in bonds of husband and wife with all manner of women and press his palms together before them.

THE THIRD-CLASS
WAITING ROOM

It took some persuasion to convince him to sit in the third-class waiting room at Tokyo Station. She had chosen that place for their rendezvous. He had resisted; she was not a woman whose life had anything to do with a place like a third-class waiting room.

"There is even a separate ladies' waiting room for first and second class. If you're in the third-class room, I won't know what to do—you'll attract attention."

"Me? Am I the sort of woman who would attract attention?"

With that, he meekly accepted her humility.

Nevertheless, despite their appointment, when he arrived at Tokyo Station, he could not go directly to the third-class waiting room. He was not that kind of man himself. Noting that it was still fifteen minutes before five o'clock, he went to the waiting room reserved for first- and second-class passengers. A movie of the scenery at Matsushima was being shown on a small screen recessed into the wall. He thought of an old friend in

Osaka and wrote a letter. Only after making a trip to the station post office with the letter could he bring himself to enter the third-class waiting room.

There was no projection screen on this wall. The third-class passengers would not be apt to go sightseeing in a place like Matsushima. A crowd of young female students from the country who appeared to be on their way home from a school trip stood chatting with each other throughout the room. He sat in their shadow as if hiding. A traditional sedge hat worn by a Buddhist pilgrim rested on the bench in front of him.

On a pilgrimage to the eighty-eight sacred sites of
Shikoku
Originally there was no east or west
Chiba Prefecture, Imba County, Shirai Village
Where is south and north
Praise the Great Teacher Buddha
We are deluded, so there are three realms
Tomizuka Hamlet
If we are enlightened, there is perfect emptiness
Kawamura Sakuji

The several lines of characters on the sedge hat still smelled of ink. The pilgrim wore white cotton under his black Buddhist robe. He peered at the colored "Shikoku Pilgrims' Map" that the priest who had come to see him off had spread out on his lap. The pilgrim nodded at each word the priest spoke, his dark glasses threatening to hide his eyebrows. The glasses did not seem suitable for an old person.

He thought about the journey to Shikoku during which the elderly man's new hat would grow old and worn. Perhaps the words

We are deluded, so there are three realms.
If we are enlightened, there is perfect emptiness.

had no connection with him. But this man, about to set out on a pilgrimage he had dreamed of for years, certainly must be happy. What a distance he sensed between the pilgrim's solitary happiness and the happiness he was anticipating. Still—he thought it over again—hadn't his own grandparents made a pilgrimage to Shikoku together? He could actually hear the tinkle of pilgrims' bells in childhood memories of his home village.

And so what of it? Irritated at having to wait for the woman, he could not dwell on it any longer.

Perhaps she was so adept at arranging lovers' secret rendezvous that she knew from experience they would attract less attention in the third-class waiting room than if they were to meet in the first-and-second-class.

Perhaps she laughed in derision at her suitors, secretly classifying them into those she arranged to meet in the first-and-second-class waiting room and those she met in the third.

Notions as foolish as these came to his mind. Imagining that she was now meeting with one of her second-class men, he glanced into the other waiting room. Wandering back, he was jostled in an avalanche of people.

The pilgrim and the priest were being led away by a policeman.

You think of me as the kind of woman who rides in
the second-class car on a train. But it's not your fault.
I usually endeavor to make myself look that way.
Yesterday when I slipped and told you to come to the
third-class waiting room, I exposed my deception. Then

at home I brooded over it. A man who would think of me as a woman who rides second-class would never work out.

This is the note he found waiting for him from the woman when he returned from Tokyo Station.

Perhaps her display of self-hatred was actually a way of ridiculing him. At any rate, he would probably live a life far removed from any third-class waiting rooms. And he would likely maintain a romantic impression of the place by preserving the scene of the pilgrim and the priest. But he could not believe that the pilgrim's garb was a criminal's disguise—as he could not believe that she was a woman who rode third-class.

THE WATCH

A lawyer who worked at a legal office had received a small sum of money for his work defending a city councilman in a bribery case. Surprisingly, he found himself an elegant girlfriend at the same time.

He invited her to the theater.

When they left the theater, they hailed a small taxi. It was the first time in his life that he had ridden in an automobile. This was a man who only six months before had avoided taking a bus in favor of being jostled along in a covered horse carriage on a trip to a hot spring.

Enclosing this bit of atmosphere inside the small cab, he tried to keep the sensation of the young woman close to him and not let it dissipate. But inside this car racing though the cold night with no sound of wind, his emotions shrank toward cowardice. He forgot where he was. He spoke absentmindedly.

"Only cheap taxis wait at that theater. But it's better to put up with this than to walk all the way to where there are high-quality cabs—it's so cold."

"Yes."

She answered curtly, then turned toward him as if to ask something, so he quickly added, "But this one rattles, and even though the cab is small, it's cold."

Then, as if to justify something to himself, he patted the stiff, uncovered leather seat. "More than anything, *this* is intolerable."

"That's right."

She failed to devise a suitable response. He sensed his own emotions turn cold with a slight edge of self-hatred.

Hoping to rescue the situation, he brazenly reached out and tried to turn over her hand, which was resting in her lap. "What time is it?"

Unexpectedly, the woman cried out sharply. "Oh, no! This watch doesn't work."

Startled, he withdrew his hand. She blushed.

"I really don't like this watch. It's too large for my thin arm. It's Japanese. Made in Japan. And besides, it's old fashioned. When did you notice I was wearing a watch? You were looking up my sleeve, weren't you?"

Dumbfounded, he could not think of anything pleasant to say.

"But it's a memento from my mother. That's why I wear it. I guess it's old fashioned to keep a memory of your mother with you."

"So, I suppose you can hear the sound of your mother."

"The sound of my mother? Yes, I suppose I can. It's Japanese made, so it makes a dull, clouded sound. Just right for a Japanese woman."

"Let me hear it."

Nonchalantly, he took her hand for the first time and lifted it to his ear. "You can hear it, can't you? Your mother is saying to you, 'Don't go out with a man.'"

The woman smiled faintly. When her arm touched his cheek he felt a shudder enter his body.

■■■

We mustn't condemn the vanity of these two. Vanity happened to give this man, who had groveled in fear of women, a little courage for love.

So, in short, as you see here, perhaps this thing called love is so absurd that it will manifest itself regardless of the means.

But, beyond that, this incident may have given this man's life a boost, a step toward living his emotions fully. Perhaps his confidence grew, merely because he had lightly touched the woman's skin.

"Let's alter the story so this elegant woman takes her gold watch to the pawn shop with the baby she has borne strapped to her back."

HISTORY

The mountain village had a highway that was much too fine for a village. However, the road's destination was not this chilly village, but a place over the mountains to the south and across the peninsula. When the road had been completed, rumors spread among the villagers. There would be a war soon. This highway was to transport guns and soldiers to the southern tip of the peninsula.

As always, the villagers had to scramble over the rocks and cross a swinging bridge to reach the hot spring beside the stream in the valley. Actually, the hot spring was in the middle of the stream rather than beside it. The tail feathers of the water birds struck the rim of the tub.

No guns came through, but automobiles passed. Then came a rich old man. The rich man said he was fond of the pure white rocks so plentiful in the river, and he built a villa. In addition to bringing water from the source to his villa, he also brought the hot water to a place under a mountain peach tree in the middle of the village and built a public bath for the villagers. He named it "Mountain Peach Bath." In the evenings, the village girls jumped at the sound of the fruit falling on the tin roof.

Then the old man built a small road along the stream. He enlarged the original spring and put in a larger concrete tub. Moreover, he bought the land along the stream where only field chrysanthemums and pampas grass grew, so the villagers were even more pleased.

About ten years later the old man began to widen the three-foot spring with explosives. Of course, it was his own land. The spring immediately began to flow poorly. The water turned lukewarm. Steam rose like the cauldron of hell from the pond that the old man had dug.

The villagers exchanged glances, and exchanged glances again. They went to the home of the old man from whom they had received so many favors. The man laughed.

"Don't worry about such things. I am going to dig a new bath for the village. I am going to make the village bath large enough for a thousand."

And that is what he did. The new bath was lined with light blue ceramic tile. The bathhouse had a twenty-mat changing room on the second floor.

In his villa, the old man wrote Chinese poetry and haiku praising the view of the stream in the valley. He enjoyed the fresh vegetables the villagers brought him. The old spring was buried under the fallen oak leaves.

When the old man died, the village erected a memorial stone for him.

The old man's son came to the unveiling. Before two weeks had passed, he began to build a hot spring inn. The public bath disappeared behind a stone wall and became the private bath for the inn.

The villagers exchanged glances, and exchanged glances again. The son scoffed at them.

The villagers replied, "You are nothing like your father. You possess nothing of your father's heart."

"Hmm. I am my father's child. I'm just not the weakling he was. I won't deceive you the way my father did."

"What a waste. We can't even bear to walk on the road the old man built."

"You worms. It's a small road just wide enough for automobiles to pass. If you were so shocked when you first realized what kind of intentions that road had, you had better open your eyes while you can and think about the intentions that lie behind that highway."

BIRTHPLACE

When the scribe who had come to rent a house saw a child of twelve or thirteen standing at the door acting like a landlord, he could not help laughing.

"Stop being a smart aleck. Just send a letter to your mother and ask her about it."

"If you ask my mother, she'll say no. You have to rent it from me."

"Then, how much is the rent?"

"Well—five yen."

"Hmm. I know the market," the scribe feigned a serious air. "Five yen is too high. Knock it down to three yen."

"Forget it." The boy appeared ready to dash off into the field out back. The scribe was trapped by this childish bargaining style. He absolutely had to have this house in front of the county office building.

"Just this month you have to pay the rent in advance."

"Do I give it to you?"

"That's right." The boy nodded with the confidence befitting a landlord. But, unable to stifle a boyish grin that welled up, he finally pursed his lips in a stiff manner. These financial transactions he had newly learned to undertake were so fun he could hardly stand it. This was his second experience in striking a deal.

His mother had gone to Tokyo to care for her oldest daughter, who was soon to give birth. She did not return during the entire month of March. She instructed the boy to come to Tokyo, but she did not send any money. The next-door neighbors look after him. When the scrap dealer called on the neighbors, the boy dragged him over to his own house and sold him old magazines and rags. The boy caught on quickly.

"Is this worth much?" He took the iron tea kettle off the charcoal brazier and showed it to the scrap man. He was increasingly absorbed with this game: anything could be sold. The boy rifled through the shabby house, even selling his late father's best clothes. If he only had five yen more, he could travel round-trip to Tokyo. These transactions made the boy feel like an adult, part of this strange life in which one is capable of obtaining one's daily provisions. But when he received the money, from the scrap dealer and the scribe, he sensed clearly the wretchedness and fatigue of their lives. Still, after these initial ventures, he felt like a winner. He knew he could survive.

The boy arrived at Ueno Station in Tokyo bearing the green scent of Aomori apples on his back. His mother was so amazed that she could not scold him. The realization that she could not return home spread through her chest like water. Her eldest son also lived in Tokyo. Though he had reproached her for years because the old house, if sold, could provide capital for his business, she could never let the house go. Now this boy had sold her husband's best clothes as though they were rags, clothes that she had saved while selling her own kimonos in order to eat.

"I'm going to sleep for three days." As soon as he arrived at his sister's house, he fell fast asleep.

His sister lived in the suburbs near a big pond. The next day the boy went fishing by himself. On the way back he brought five or six children with him and was dividing up the fourteen carp at the gate of the house.

Inside the house, the mother and daughter cried. The daughter's husband had decided to send the boy to apprentice with a plasterer he knew from work; the man was to call for the boy that evening. The mother protested that she would take the boy back to the country rather than send him away as an apprentice. The boy leapt up, and spoke as though he were jumping over a puddle.

"If you are going to argue and cry so much, I'll gladly go anywhere as an apprentice."

Silently, the mother began to darn the boy's socks. The boy had brought his mother's unlined kimonos and his own belongings, and, even though summer was approaching, he had brought his winter socks, stuffed in a wicker trunk.

BURNING
THE PINE BOUGHS

It was still the first week of the new year, but the temperature in Atami was in the seventies for two days, as though it were early summer. The newspaper ran a photograph of plum blossoms in a park in Tokyo with a caption that read "Plums deceived into blooming." Apparently Tokyo was warm, too. I, on the other hand, caught a cold. When I went outside after the two warm days, a bitter chill ran down my spine.

On the thirteenth I went to sleep in the late afternoon. By the time I woke up and ate supper, it was past ten o'clock. I played go with Okayo. I had a fever, so every wrong move she made grated on my nerves.

"You're so dumb. And you always said you wanted to study—with a head like yours."

Okayo looked crestfallen and said nothing. She had not yet graduated from secondary girls school but still hoped to get a secondary education. Surely she did not need to have her hopes battered from across the board just because she was not good at go.

She regained her spirits but kept silent. It was nearly two o'clock when she said we should go to bed. But first, she got into the bath.

"Listen. Listen. Be quiet. He's back again." She shrank down into the bath in fear. There was a sound on the roof.

"Listen."

I held my breath and kept still as I was told, but I could not hear anything there.

"If it's going to be like this here, let's move at the end of the month."

"Yes, let's do."

If, as had happened the other day, a thief was going to peek through the skylight in the kitchen, then he would first creep onto the roof over the bath. One just can't live this way. We never thought that the young rascal of a thief who came the other day would be brazen enough to come a second time. And it was too coincidental that a different thief would target the same house. Still, ever since then, Okayo was terrified even to step into the kitchen after nightfall. Late at night I, too, listened for wood creaking here and there in the house.

In all my life I had never imagined that a thief would break into a house of mine, but once it happened, I perpetually felt like a target. "When you see a stranger, consider him a thief." Okayo seemed to have taken this old saying to heart. When we walked around town, I would often look into the face of a boy I happened to notice and ask her laughingly, "Do you think that's him?"

One stormy night two or three days before, when we were at a movie, I noticed that the boy sitting next to me looked just like the thief from the other night. It was not just my eyes playing tricks; his profile in the dim light closely resembled that of the thief.

"What an unexpected meeting!" I thought to myself. I could not help smiling, sensing something like a trick of fate. When the lights came up, I saw he was wearing a middle-school uniform. He had lovely hands. I did not remember the kid from the other night having such beautiful hands.

Anyway, in view of these strange occurrences, I could not laugh off Okayo's fear.

After I went upstairs to bed, Okayo spoke.

"Let's stay up a little longer." I had slept until ten, so I wasn't tired anyway.

"Listen. Listen. That sound. Someone's here, don't you think?"

Indeed, there was a noise from the roof. If you listened, it really did sound as though someone were tiptoeing on the roof. When I thought Okayo was finally asleep, she awoke from a nightmare.

"Someone came in and was standing by my pillow. My head grew numb, and I couldn't move, . . ." she continued.

"Hey." A little later, it was I who shook Okayo awake. "What's that sound? That banging. You hear it, don't you?"

"If that's what you're talking about, I've been listening to it for a while," Okayo said.

"Isn't someone hammering on the lattice door beside the entryway?" I said.

"I think so."

It did sound as though someone were hammering on wood. I got up, opened the peephole on the shutters, and looked out. There was no sign of anyone in the garden. I could see into the glass door of the inn across the way. Three or four rats were scampering about on the wooden floor. What we had thought was the sound of hammering was the beating of a drum in the distance.

"It's a drum." I got back in bed and tried to sleep, but the drumbeat grew louder. It grew closer, too, as if someone were beating wildly through the streets of the town.

"That's funny. I wonder if there's a forest fire."

"Maybe."

"But if there were a forest fire, the alarm would sound. I wonder if it's a thief. Maybe they're waking up the town in order to catch a thief."

There seemed to be more than one or two drums. We could hear the shouts of a crowd amid the random beating.

"Maybe it *is* a forest fire. Or a riot. Or maybe Tokyo is on fire. Or robbers have come to attack Atami."

We even heard a pistol shot amid the shouts and drumbeats. Perhaps a thief surrounded by the townspeople had fired a pistol.

"I think I'll go see what it is," I said.

"Don't."

"I wonder what's going on."

"Isn't it some kind of event—like a festival?"

Come to think of it, the cries did sound like chanting, as though people were carrying a shrine palanquin around.

"But it would be strange to run around waking up the whole town even if it were a festival," I said.

"It's probably a ship in distress."

"On a night like this, with no wind?"

"I suppose not."

"I wonder if a hot spring has erupted."

I got up again and peeked outside. There was fire and smoke on a hill off to the right.

"There's a fire burning."

"So it must be a ship in trouble."

"But then the fire would be closer to the shore."

For some reason, the sound of the drum invigorated us.

"You're not scared anymore, are you, with everyone up making such a racket?"

"No, I'm not." Her voice was brighter.

After a while, Okayo spoke casually. "Shall we separate?"

"That would be all right. What would you do after we parted?"

"I would rent a house with my younger sister. I'd send her to school, and I'd go to night school myself. I'd work somewhere during the day. And you would have to send me some money every month."

"How much?"

"I think seventy yen would be enough."

"What would you do after you graduated from girls school? You can't do anything with just a degree from a girls school."

"I'll study more."

"What?"

"History and Japanese."

"Hmmm. Then you'd become a teacher at a girls school?"

"No, I don't want to do that."

The two of us calculated in detail whether she and her sister could live on seventy yen a month.

And just as if we were characters in a fairy tale, she asked me, "What are you going to do?"

"Well, I guess I'll live in a boardinghouse."

"Then I'll take the utensils in the kitchen."

"I'll give you things like that. If I had some money, I'd buy some public bonds. Then I could earn a premium off them of two thousand yen."

Okayo fell into a peaceful sleep. I could hear the long sound of a horn coming from the ocean. Maybe it was a ship in distress after all. The beating of the drum continued. By now the sky over the ocean was probably beginning to whiten with the morning light.

It would be lonely and cold once I left Okayo and began living in a boardinghouse. Maybe I would travel, and when I returned, Okayo would put me up at her place. But Okayo's talk about breaking up without any explanation—that's why it seemed like a fairy tale—was pleasing for me, like watching a captive deer escape to the mountains. Her idea that life would be more mean-ingful for her alone—with an education rather than with a man—was interesting. Moreover, the fact that she was thinking so independently lightened my spirits.

I got up and went to the parlor, where the noon sun shone in. Okayo appeared. She had been doing laundry.

"They said that the drum last night was for the burn-ing of the pine boughs that are used to decorate the gate for New Year's."

"Oh."

"They told me the children in the town gather every year and burn them. They beat the drum around the town to inform the people that it is not a house fire. It was the day set aside for the god of children who have died. The children's spirits build cairns of rocks in the river bottoms as memorials for their own dead parents, but demons knock them down, or something like that. The custom used to be observed during the Bon festival, but nowadays the teachers at school complain too much. It's become a yearly event in Atami."

"That's interesting. But they didn't burn our pine boughs for us, did they?"

The children come by at the end of the year to collect

donations to offer to the god of the dead children's spirits. Then at New Year's they come to collect the pine
decorations. I had not understood what was happening,
so I had turned them away. Anyway, when I went outside to check, there were no pine boughs on our gate.

"So our decorations are gone, too! I wonder when
they took them?"

"I wonder."

Somehow I felt happy.

A PRAYER IN
THE MOTHER TONGUE

1

He was reading a book on linguistics.

This was a fact reported by a Dr. Rush, an American.

There was an Italian by the name of Professor Scandila. He was a teacher of Italian, French, and English. He died of yellow fever.

On the day the fever began, he was speaking English. About midway through his illness, he spoke only French. And finally, in his last hours, he spoke only his native Italian. Naturally, it was not that he, delirious with fever, had had the presence of mind to do it just for show.

And this happened to an Italian woman who was temporarily insane.

After she first went crazy, she spoke very poor Italian.

Then, as she got worse, she spoke French. After her illness began to abate, she used German. And when she was finally recovering, she returned to her native Italian.

An elderly government forester, who had lived on the Polish border as a boy, spent the rest of his life in Germany. For thirty or forty years he neither spoke Polish nor ever heard it, so you might assume he had completely forgotten the language.

However, during the two hours he was under anesthesia, he spoke, prayed, and sang, all in Polish.

Among Dr. Rush's acquaintances was a German who had worked for many years as a missionary for the Lutheran Church in Philadelphia. He told the following story to Rush.

There were some old Swedish people in the southern part of the city. Some fifty or sixty years had passed since they had immigrated to the United States. During that time they had seldom spoken in Swedish, so seldom in fact that no one thought they still remembered it.

Nevertheless, many of the people, when they were on their deathbeds, about to draw their last breath, prayed in Swedish, their mother tongue, their long buried memories returning as though from a great distance.

This is a story about language. But what does this mystery tell us?

"That sort of occurrence is nothing more than an aberration of the memory." A psychologist would be likely to respond thus.

But a sentimentalist would, with sentimental arms, embrace the old people, who could not help but pray in their mother tongue.

If that is so, then what is language? Just a code. What is a mother tongue?

"Linguistic differences developed among barbaric tribes

as a means for one tribe to hide its secrets from others."

There was even a book that said that. If so, then a prayer in the mother tongue, far from being an old human convention to which we are inextricably bound, is perhaps a means of emotional support. Humankind, with its long history, is by now a corpse bound to a tree with the ropes of convention. If the ropes were cut, the corpse would simply fall to the ground. Prayer in one's mother tongue is a manifestation of that pathetic state.

Even so—but no, he felt that way because he was reading a linguistics book and remembered Kayoko.

"Perhaps Kayoko is something like a mother tongue to me."

2

"Its breast is not as broad as a dove's, but its wings when spread are as wide as a dove's."

This was the description of a grasshopper. When he awoke, these words lingered in his mind. He had dreamed about a giant grasshopper.

He could not remember anything before that. Anyway, a huge grasshopper was flying about, batting its wings by his ear, no, almost touching his cheek. He understood clearly what sort of method he should use to break with Kayoko. The grasshopper had instructed him.

In one moment he was striding down a country road. It must have been nighttime. He could barely distinguish the sparse trees along the way. The big dovelike grasshopper dodged about his cheeks. There was no sound. Strangely enough, he felt exalted by the beating of the wings. He touched the secret teachings of esoteric Buddhism in the pulse of the wingbeats. In other words, the dovelike grasshopper was an apostle of Truth. It was morally correct to leave Kayoko. This grasshopper had taught him of morality.

With this in mind, he hurried down the milk-colored road as though somehow he were being followed. The moment the description of the grasshopper came to mind, he woke up.

"Its breast is not as broad as a dove's, but its wings when spread are as wide as a dove's."

The doubled-flowered tuberose smelled white at his bedside. It was a July flower. That is why the grasshoppers were not chirping yet. So why had he dreamed of a grasshopper? Had something occurred in the past to connect Kayoko with grasshoppers?

Surely, he and Kayoko had heard grasshoppers chirping in the suburbs. And perhaps they had also seen them flying as they walked together in the autumn fields. Nevertheless—

"Why would the beating of a grasshopper's wings be a symbol of morality?"

That is the way it is with dreams. Yet he could not unearth a memory of grasshoppers to help him analyze his dream. He smiled and fell back asleep.

By the skylight above the large entryway of a farmer's house was a room like a swallow's nest. The room was built like a tower. He had concealed himself in this mysterious nest.

But something made him restless; he could not keep still for long in this attic hiding place.

He slid like an acrobat down a bamboo pole to the inner garden. As before, a man was following him. He fled out the back gate—the house belonged to his uncle in the country.

Out in the back there was a tiny boy, like Issunboshi of the fairy tale, blocking his way as he tried to run into the rice storehouse.

"No. No. You cannot hide in a place like that."

"Then tell me where I *can* hide."

"Go hide in the bath."

"The bath?"

"There is no other place but the bathroom. Hurry. Hurry."

The boy urged him to take off his clothes. He thought there might be trouble if the other man found the boy holding the clothes, but he scrambled through the window into the bathroom. What a surprise! What touched him like warm water was Kayoko's skin. She had climbed in ahead of him. Her skin was smooth, as though oiled. The tub was so small that the two of them could not fit in together.

"This won't work. If that man discovers us like this, there will be no end to the suspicions that will surround us."

The sensation of Kayoko against his skin and his terror woke him up.

The gold design on his wife's lacquered headrest sparkled. The lamps were out and the morning light was filtering in. He groped for his wife's body. She was wrapped in her sleeping robe all the way to her feet.

So it was not the touch of his wife's body that had caused a dream like this.

Anyway, who was this man who was trying to kill him in his dream? It was certainly Kayoko's husband or lover. But she had never been with another man when they parted, so he would never have seen or heard of him. He wondered why he would dream of being chased by some man.

Had the affair with Kayoko made him so conceited that he thought he could be the object of someone's jealousy? Perhaps. Even now he had to be taught by the grasshopper that his break with her was moral. Maybe because it was not.

3

"I'm Kayoko's uncle."

The man stepped up into the house as if he needed to say no more than this to be granted entry.

"Actually, the reason I've come here is that Kayoko sent me a peculiar letter, so I wanted to meet you once and talk."

The uncle cast a suspicious glance at the man's wife as she served tea.

"If she's here, would you call her?" the uncle asked.

"You mean Kayoko?"

"Yes."

"I have no idea where she is."

"I'm vaguely aware of the circumstances. Please don't conceal anything. I received a letter. It was sent from your address." The uncle pulled a letter from his pocket. Kagawa Prefecture was written on the front. He wondered if her uncle had come all the way to Tokyo from Kayoko's hometown on the island of Shikoku just to see him. And the return address said it was indeed from Kayoko care of his present address. Startled, he checked the postmark; it had been sent from the post office in Atami District where he lived.

"Please read it."

Dear Uncle,
I have left all of my affairs up to Mr. Kitani. My fate
and my funeral. And so please forgive me if not even
a lock of my hair ever returns to my hometown. If
you have a chance, please see Mr. Kitani and ask him
about it. I wonder what he will say about me.
                                        Kayoko
                             Care of Mr. Kitani

What sort of riddle was this? How did she know
where he lived? Why had she come here to the coast?
Was it just to mail this letter?

Two days later there was a rumor that a fisherman
from Uomi Cape had discovered a lovers' double suicide.
People said that from the top of a three-hundred-foot
cliff the fisherman had seen the bodies on the ocean
floor as distinctly as fish in an aquarium. Perhaps the
water was unusually clear for early summer.

"It's Kayoko."

It was natural that his intuition should prove correct.
She had chosen his town for the site of her suicide.
The face on the man's body was expressionless. But this
man had envied Kayoko's first lover, even in the moment
of his death.

As death approaches, memory erodes. Recent memories are the first to succumb. Death works its way
backward until it reaches memory's earliest beginnings.
Then memory flares up for an instant, just like a flame
about to go out. That is the "prayer in the mother
tongue."

And so, what burned in Kayoko's heart as she died in
the water was not her partner in suicide but the face of

her first lover. Perhaps that was her pathetic prayer in the mother tongue.

"What a stupid woman."

He spoke to her uncle with such irritation and anger you would think he wanted to kick the body. Perhaps he was talking to himself.

"Until she died, she was possessed by an old ghost. She was with me for a mere two years, but she never could escape me. She made herself a slave for life. A damned prayer in the mother tongue!"

THE SETTING SUN

A nearsighted woman was hurriedly writing a card in the garden of a small post office.

"The train window—the train window—the train window." She wrote this three times, then erased it and wrote: "Now—now—now."

The special-delivery agent scratched his head with a pencil.

A waitress in a large restaurant was having the cook tie her new apron in the kitchen.

"Are you going to make me tie it in the back? The back is the past, isn't it? Let me tie it in the front at your breasts."

"What!"

The poet bought sugar, too. The shop boy at the sugar store stuck the big scoop into a mound of sugar.

"No, I've decided I'm not going to go home and cook rice cakes. If I put sugar in my pocket and walk through the town, maybe some white daydreams will drift into my mind."

Then the poet whispered to the crowds who passed him.

"Hey, you people. You are going toward the past. I'm walking toward the future. Is there anyone who will walk the same direction as me? Naturally, to the future? Of course not."

The post-office boy's bicycle circled the nearsighted woman.

"Hello, hello."

"Oh, I'm nearsighted. I can't even see the pure white sugar at the sugar shop. I thought I saw him and that woman in the window of the train, but perhaps . . . Maybe he is wondering about me now . . . If . . . Oh, Mr. Special Delivery Man!"

The poet and the waitress smiled in the restaurant.

"That's a new apron, isn't it? Let me see the back— that new white butterfly sitting there."

"No. Don't look at my past."

"That's all right. I came upon you while I was walking toward the future."

Then the sun, which had been caught until that moment on the roof of the pawn shop's storehouse at the end of the street running from east to west, slipped down without a sound.

Ah. In that instant all the people walking on the street sighed a bit and slackened their pace by three steps. But they did not notice that they had done so.

However, the children playing at the east end of the street looked to the west. They all crouched down, braced themselves, and jumped. They were trying to catch sight of the sun.

"I can see it!"

"I can see it!"

"I can see it!"

"You're lying. You can't see it at all—"

Printed in the United States
by Baker & Taylor Publisher Services